TALES
OF
POLYNESIA

TALES OF POLYNESIA

FOLKTALES FROM

Hawai'i, New Zealand, Tahiti, and Samoa

ILLUSTRATIONS BY

Yiling Changues

CHRONICLE BOOKS
SAN FRANCISCO

Library of Congress Cataloging-in-Publication Data
Names: Changues, Yiling, illustrator.
Title: Tales of Polynesia : folktales from Hawaiʻi, New Zealand, Tahiti, and Samoa / illustrations by Yiling Changues.
Description: San Francisco, California : Chronicle Books, [2023] | Includes bibliographical references.
Identifiers: LCCN 2022032981 | ISBN 9781797217567 (Hardcover)
Subjects: LCSH: Folklore--Polynesia. | Legends--Hawaii. | Legends--New Zealand. | Legends--Tahiti. | Legends--Samoa.
Classification: LCC GR380 .T35 2023 | DDC 398.20996--dc23/eng/20220719
LC record available at https://lccn.loc.gov/2022032981

Manufactured in China.

Design by Jon Glick.
Illustrations by Yiling Changues.
Sensitivity read by Sloane Leong.

10 9 8 7 6 5 4 3 2 1

Chronicle books and gifts are available at special quantity discounts to corporations, professional associations, literacy programs, and other organizations. For details and discount information, please contact our premiums department at corporatesales@chroniclebooks.com or at 1-800-759-0190.

Chronicle Books LLC
680 Second Street
San Francisco, California 94107
www.chroniclebooks.com

"[T]o the north lies a rocky islet covered with shrubs. Near this insulated mass of rhyolite there is a cave with a rock-arched entrance, half-screened by bushes and ferns. It is a story-cave, a refuge place of long ago."

—James Cowan and Hon. Sir Maui Pomare,
"Tunohopu's Cave: A Tale of Old Rotorua"

CONTENTS

LIFE AND DEATH

FAMILY

SOURCES

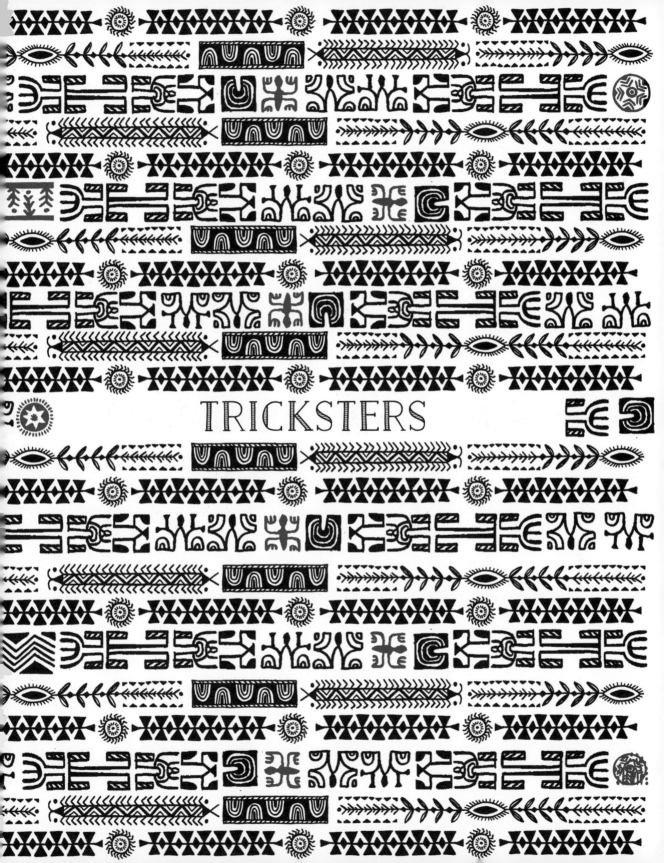

TRICKSTERS

THE LEGEND of PAIHE OTUU

Tahiti

Paihe otuu was an audacious little heron who, as the legend goes, devoured a gigantic heron who lived in a cave in Raiatea.

They called him Otuu nunamu, and he had kidnapped the wife of Tuoropaa. The latter, who was king, sent messengers all around Raiatea and Tahaa to gather all the herons and lead them to war against Otuu nunamu.

But they all feared to attack the giant, and they were returning each one to his island, islet, or patch of coral when they met the little Paihe otuu.

"Where have you been?" they asked him. They explained to him the situation.

"And why return instead of going to fight Otuu nunamu?"

"He's so large," they said, "that at the mere thought of attacking him, fear ties our stomachs in knots."

"Right," said Paihe otuu, "now it's his stomach that I'll tie in knots." And he flew off toward the giant's hideout.

He arrived and perched on Otuu nunamu's beak. The big heron tried to shake him off and opened his beak, and the little heron slipped inside, descended his throat, and calmly began to devour his intestines.

"Oh! Oh!" cried the immense bird. "What is this pain inside me? I've swallowed up the whale, the dolphin, the porpoise, the black fish, the shark, the tuna, I've gulped down entire shoals of mackerel, but I've never felt a pain like this." He made an effort and expulsed Paihe otuu, who was sent flying all the way to Tahaa.

When he recovered from the shock, the little heron went to bathe in the river and then returned to the fight. Once again, he perched on the beak of the giant and in the same way penetrated his stomach.

Expulsed several times, he went back tirelessly and, in the end, completely devoured the enormous bird's intestines.

Then he freed the wife of Tuoropaa and returned her to her husband.

All the herons gathered and proclaimed him king. "This little heron is a great warrior," they said, "because on his own, he triumphed in a fight that all the herons did not even dare take on."

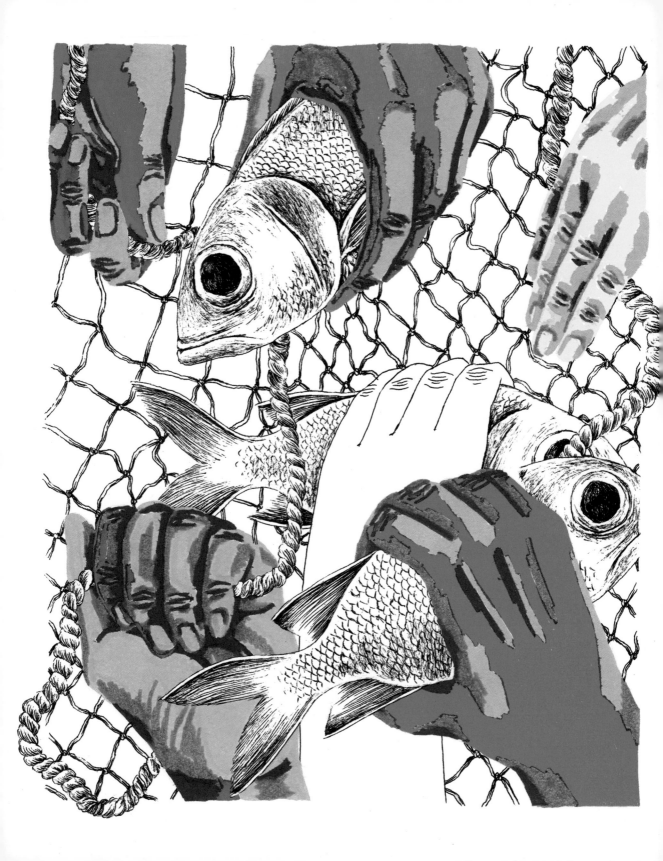

THE ART of NETTING LEARNED by KAHUKURA from the FAIRIES
(*Ko Te Korero Mo Nga Patupaiarehe*)

꙳꙳꙳꙳꙳

New Zealand

Once upon a time, a man of the name of Kahukura wished to pay a visit to Rangiaowhia, a place lying far to the northward, near the country of the tribe called Te Rarawa. Whilst he lived at his own village, he was continually haunted by a desire to visit that place. At length he started on his journey, and reached Rangiaowhia, and as he was on his road, be passed a place where some people had been cleaning mackerel, and he saw the inside of the fish lying all about the sand on the seashore: surprised at this, he looked about at the marks, and said to himself, "Oh, this must have been done by some of the people of the district." But when he came to look a little more narrowly at the footmarks, he saw that the people who had been fishing had made them in the night-time, not that morning, nor in the day; and he said to himself, "These are no mortals who have been fishing here—spirits must have done this; had they been men, some of the reeds and grass which they sat on in their canoe would have been lying about." He felt quite sure from several circumstances, that spirits or fairies had been there; and after observing everything well, he returned to the house where he was stopping. He, however, held fast in his heart what he had seen, as something very striking to tell all his friends in every direction, and as likely to be the means of gaining knowledge which might enable him to find out something new.

So that night he returned to the place where he had observed all these things, and just as he reached the spot, back had come the fairies too, to haul their net for mackerel; and some of them were shouting out, "The net here! The net here!" Then a canoe paddled off to fetch the other in which the net was laid, and as they dropped the net into the water, they began to cry out, "Drop the net in the sea at Rangiaowhia, and haul it at Mamaku." These words were sung out by the fairies, as an encouragement in their work and from the joy of their hearts at their sport in fishing.

As the fairies were dragging the net to the shore, Kahukura managed to mix amongst them, and hauled away at the rope; he happened to be a very fair man, so that his skin was almost as white as that of these fairies, and from that cause he was not observed by them. As the net came close in to the shore, the fairies began to cheer and shout, "Go out into the sea some of you, in front of the rocks, lest the nets should be entangled at Tawatawauia by Teweteweuia'," for that was the name of a rugged rock standing out from the sandy shore; the main body of the fairies kept hauling at the net, and Kahukura pulled away in the midst of them.

When the first fish reached the shore, thrown up in the ripples driven before the net as they hauled it in, the fairies had not yet remarked Kahukura, for he was almost as fair as they were. It was just at the very first peep of dawn that the fish were all landed, and the fairies ran hastily to pick them up from the sand, and to haul the net up on the beach. They did not act with their fish as men do, dividing them into separate loads for each, but every one took up what fish he liked, and ran a twig through their gills, and as they strung the fish, they continued calling out, "Make haste, run here, all of you, and finish the work before the sun rises."

Kahukura kept on stringing his fish with the rest of them. He had only a very short string, and, making a slipknot at the end of it, when he had covered the string with fish, he lifted them up, but had hardly raised them from the ground when the slip-knot gave way from the weight of the fish, and off they fell; then some of the fairies ran good-naturedly to help him to string his fish again, and one of them tied the knot at the end of the string for him, but the fairy had hardly gone after knotting it, before Kahukura had unfastened it, and again tied a slip-knot at the end; then he began stringing his fish again, and when he had got a great many on, up he lifted them, and off they slipped as before. This trick he repeated several times, and delayed the fairies in their work by getting them to knot his string for him, and put his fish on it. At last full daylight broke, so that there was light enough to distinguish a man's face, and the fairies saw that Kahukura was a man; then they dispersed in confusion, leaving their fish and their net, and abandoning their canoes, which were nothing but stems of the flax. In a moment the fairies started for their own abodes; in their hurry, as has just been said, they abandoned their net, which was made of rushes; and off the good people fled as fast as they could go. Now was first discovered the stitch for netting a net, for they left theirs with Kahukura, and it became a pattern for him. He thus taught his children to make nets, and by them the Māori race were made acquainted with that art, which they have now known from very remote times.

THE TWO SORCERERS
(*Ko Te Matenga O Kiki*)

New Zealand

Kiki was a celebrated sorcerer, and skilled in magical arts; he lived upon the river Waikato. The inhabitants of that river still have this proverb, "The offspring of Kiki wither shrubs." This proverb had its origin in the circumstance of Kiki being such a magician, that he could not go abroad in the sunshine; for if his shadow fell upon any place not protected from his magic, it at once became tapu, and all the plants there withered.

This Kiki was thoroughly skilled in the practice of sorcery. If any parties coming up the river called at his village in their canoes as they paddled by, he still remained quietly at home, and never troubled himself to come out, but just drew back the sliding door of his house, so that it might stand open, and the strangers stiffened and died; or even as canoes came paddling down from the upper parts of the river, he drew back the sliding wooden shutter to the window of his house, and the crews on board of them were sure to die.

At length, the fame of this sorcerer spread exceedingly, and resounded through every tribe, until Tamure, a chief who dwelt at Kawhia, heard with others, reports of the magical powers of Kiki, for his fame extended over the whole country. At length Tamure thought he would go and contend in the arts of sorcery with Kiki, that it might be seen which of them was most skilled in magic; and he arranged in his own mind a fortunate season for his visit.

When this time came, he selected two of his people as his companions, and he took his young daughter with him also; and they all crossed over the mountain range from Kawhia, and came down upon the river Waipa, which runs into the Waikato, and embarking there in a canoe, paddled down the river towards the village of Kiki; and they managed so well, that before they were seen by anybody, they had arrived at the landing-place. Tamure was not only skilled in magic, but he was also a very cautious man; so whilst they were still afloat upon the river, he repeated an incantation of the kind called "Mata-tawhito," to preserve him safe from all arts of sorcery; and he repeated other incantations, to ward off spells, to protect him from magic, to collect good genii round him, to keep off evil spirits, and to shield him from demons; when these preparations were all finished, they landed, and drew up their canoe on the beach, at the landing-place of Kiki.

As soon as they had landed, the old sorcerer called out to them that they were welcome to his village, and invited them to come up to it; so they went up to the village: and when they reached the square in the centre, they seated themselves upon the ground; and some of Kiki's people kindled fire in an enchanted oven, and began to cook food in it for the strangers. Kiki sat in his house, and Tamure on the ground just outside the entrance to it, and he there availed himself of this opportunity to repeat incantations over the threshold of the house, so that Kiki might be enchanted as he stepped over it to come out. When the food in the enchanted oven was cooked, they pulled off the coverings, and spread it out upon clean mats. The old sorcerer now made his appearance out of his house, and he invited Tamure to come and eat food with him; but the food was all enchanted, and his object in asking Tamure to eat with him was, that the enchanted food might kill him; therefore Tamure said that his young daughter was very hungry, and would eat of the food offered to them; he in the meantime kept on repeating incantations of the kind called Mata-tawhito, Whakangungu, and Parepare, protections against enchanted food, and as she ate she also contin-ued to repeat them; even when she stretched out her hand to take a sweet potato, or any other food, she dropped the greater part of it at her feet, and hid it under her clothes, and then only ate a little bit. After she had done, the old sorcerer, Kiki, kept waiting for Tamure to begin to eat also of the enchanted food, that he might soon die. Kiki having gone into his house again, Tamure still sat on the ground outside the door, and as he had enchanted the threshold of the house, he now repeated incantations which might render the door enchanted also, so that Kiki might be certain not to escape when he passed out of it. By this time Tamure's daughter had quite finished her meal, but neither her father nor either of his people had partaken of the enchanted food.

Tamure now ordered his people to launch his canoe, and they paddled away, and a little time after they had left the village, Kiki became unwell; in the meanwhile, Tamure and his people were paddling homewards in all haste, and as they passed a village where there were a good many people on the river's bank, Tamure stopped, and said to them, "If you should see any canoe pulling after us, and the people in the canoe ask you, have you seen a canoe pass up the river, would you be good enough to say, 'Yes, a canoe has passed by here?' and then, if they ask you, 'How far has it got?' would you be good enough to say, 'Oh, by this time it has got very far up the river?'" and having thus said to the people of that village, Tamure paddled away again in his canoe with all haste.

Some time after Tamure's party had left the village of Kiki, the old sorcerer became very ill indeed, and his people then knew that this had been brought about by the magical arts of Tamure, and they sprang into a canoe to follow after him, and pulled up the river as hard as they could; and when they reached the village where the people were on the river's bank, they called out and asked them, "How far has the canoe reached, which passed up the river?" and the villagers answered, "Oh, that canoe must got very far up the river by this time." The people in the canoe that was pursuing Tamure, upon hearing this, returned again to their own village, and Kiki died from the incantations of Tamure.

Some of Kiki's descendants are still living—one of them, named Mokahi, recently died at Tauranga-a-Ruru, but Te Maioha is still living on the river Waipa. Yes, some of the descendants of Kiki, whose shadow withered trees, are still living. He was indeed a great sorcerer: He overcame every other sorcerer until he met Tamure, but he was vanquished by him, and had to bend the knee before him.

Tamure has also some descendants living, amongst whom are Mahu and Kiake of the Ngati-Mariu tribe; these men are also skilled in magic: if a father skilled in magic died, he left his incantations to his children; so that if a man was skilled in sorcery, it was known that his children would have a good knowledge of the same arts, as they were certain to have derived it from their parent.

THE LEGEND of RATA:
HIS ADVENTURES with the
ENCHANTED TREE and REVENGE
of HIS FATHER'S MURDER

New Zealand

Before Tawhaki ascended up into the heavens, a son named Wahieroa had been born to him by his first wife. As soon as Wahieroa grew to man's estate, he took Kura for a wife, and she bore him a son whom they called Rata. Wahieroa was slain treacherously by a chief named Matukutakotako, but his son Rata was born some time before his death. It therefore became his duty to revenge the death of his father Wahieroa, and Rata having grown up, at last devised a plan for doing this; he therefore gave the necessary orders to his dependants, at the same time saying to them, "I am about to go in search of the man who slew my father."

He then started upon a journey for this purpose, and at length arrived at the entrance to the place of Matukutakotako; he found there a man who was left in charge of it, sitting at the entrance to the courtyard, and he asked him, saying, "Where is the man who killed my father?" The man who was left in charge of the place answered him, "He lives beneath in the earth there, and I am left here by him, to call to him and warn him when the new moon appears; at that season he rises and comes forth upon the earth and devours men as his food."

Rata then said to him, "All that you say is true, but how can he know when the proper time comes for him to rise up from the earth?" The man replied, "I call aloud to him."

Then said Rata, "When will there be a new moon?" And the man who was left to take care of the place answered him, "In two nights hence. Do you now return to your own village, but on the morning of the second day from this time come here again to me."

Rata, in compliance with these directions, returned to his own dwelling, and waited there until the time that had been appointed him, and on the morning of that day he again journeyed along the road he had previously travelled, and found the man sitting in the same place, and he asked him, saying, "Do you know any spot where I can conceal myself, and lie hid from the enemy with whom I am about to fight, from Matukutakotako?" The man replied, "Come with me until I show you the two fountains of clear water."

They then went together until they came to the two fountains.

The man then said to Rata, "The spot that we stand on is the place where Matuku rises up from the earth, and yonder fountain is the one in which he combs and washes his dishevelled hair, but this fountain is the one he uses to reflect his face in whilst he dresses it; you cannot kill him whilst he is at the fountain he uses to reflect his face in, because your shadow would be also reflected in it, and he would see it; but at the fountain in which he washes his hair, you may smite and slay him."

Rata then asked the man, "Will he make his appearance from the earth this evening?" And the man answered, "Yes."

They had not waited long there, when evening arrived, and the moon became visible, and the man said to Rata, "Do you now go and hide yourself near the brink of the fountain in which he washes his hair"; and Rata went and hid himself near the edge of the fountain, and the man who had been left to watch for the purpose shouted aloud, "Ho, ho, the new moon is visible—a moon two days old." And Matukutakotako heard him, and seizing his two-handed wooden sword, he rose up from the earth there, and went straight to his two fountains; then he laid down his two-handed wooden sword on the ground, at the edge of the fountain where he dressed his hair, and kneeling down on both knees beside it, he loosened the strings which bound up his long locks, and shook out his dishevelled hair, and plunged down his head into the cool clear waters of the fountain. So Rata, creeping out from where he lay hid, rapidly moved up, and stood behind him, and as Matukutakotako raised his head from the water, Rata, with one hand seized him by the hair, while with the other he smote and slew him; thus he avenged the death of his father Wahieroa.

Rata then asked the man whom he had found in charge of the place, "Where shall I find the bones of Wahieroa, my father?" And the keeper of the place answered him, "They are not here; a strange people who live at a distance came and carried them off."

Upon bearing this Rata returned to his own village, and there reflected over many designs by which he might recover the bones of his father.

At length he thought of an excellent plan for this purpose, so he went into the forest and having found a very tall tree, quite straight throughout its entire length, he felled it, and cut off its noble branching top, intending to fashion the trunk into a canoe; and all the insects which inhabit trees, and the spirits of the forests, were very angry at this, and as soon as Rata had returned to the village at evening, when his day's work was ended, they all came and took the tree, and raised it up again, and the innumerable multitude of insects, birds, and spirits, who are called "The offspring of Hakuturi," worked away at replacing each little chip and shaving in its proper place, and sang aloud their incantations as they worked; this was what they sang with a confused noise of various voices:

> Fly together, chips and shavings,
> Stick ye fast together,
> Hold ye fast together;
> Stand upright again, O tree!

Early the next morning back came Rata, intending to work at hewing the trunk of his tree into a canoe. When he got to the place where he had left the trunk lying on the ground, at first he could not find it, and if that fine tall straight tree, which he saw standing whole and sound in the forest, was the same he thought he had cut down, there it was now erect again; however, he stepped up to it, and manfully hewing away at it again, he felled it to the ground once more, and off he cut its fine branching top again, and began to hollow out the hold of the canoe, and to slope off its prow and the stern into their proper gracefully curved forms; and in the evening, when it became too dark to work, he returned to his village.

As soon as he was gone, back came the innumerable multitudes of insects, birds, and spirits, who are called the offspring of Hakuturi, and they raised up the tree upon its stump once more, and with a confused noise of various voices, they sang incantations as they worked, and when they had ended these, the tree again stood sound as ever in its former place in the forest.

The morning dawned, and Rata returned once more to work at his canoe. When he reached the place, was not he amazed to see the tree standing up in the forest, untouched, just as he had at first found it? But he, nothing daunted, hews away at it again, and down it topples, crashing to the earth; as soon as he saw the tree upon the ground, Rata went off as if going home, and then turned back and hid himself in the underwood, in a spot whence he could peep out and see what took place; he had not been hidden long, when he heard the innumerable multitude of the children of Tane approaching the spot, singing their incantations as they came along; at last they arrived close to the place where the tree was lying upon the ground. Lo, a rush upon them is made by Rata. Ha, he has seized some of them; he shouts out to them, saying, "Ha, ha, it is you, is it, then, who have been exercising your magical arts upon my tree?" Then the children of Tane all cried aloud in reply, "Who gave you authority to fell the forest god to the ground? You had no right to do so."

When Rata heard them say this, he was quite overcome with shame at what he had done.

The offspring of Tane again all called out aloud to him—"Return, O Rata, to thy village, we will make a canoe for you."

Rata, without delay, obeyed their orders, and as soon as he had gone they all fell to work; they were so numerous, and understood each what to do so well, that they no sooner began to adze out a canoe than it was completed. When they had done this, Rata and his tribe lost no time in hauling it from the forest to the water, and the name they gave to that canoe was Riwaru.

When the canoe was afloat upon the sea, 140 warriors embarked on board it, and without delay they paddled off to seek their foes; one night, just at nightfall, they reached the fortress of their enemies who were named Ponaturi. When they arrived there, Rata alone landed, leaving the canoe afloat and all his warriors on board; as he stole along the shore, he saw that a fire was burning on the sacred place, where the Ponaturi consulted their gods and offered sacrifices to them. Rata, without stopping, crept directly towards the fire, and hid himself behind some thick bushes of the Harakeke;[1] he then saw that there were some priests upon the other side of the same bushes, serving at the sacred place, and, to assist themselves in their magical arts, they were making use of the bones of Wahieroa, knocking them together to beat time while they were repeating a powerful incantation, known only to themselves, the name of which was Titikura. Rata listened attentively to this incantation, until he learnt it by heart, and when he was quite sure that he knew it, he rushed suddenly upon the priests; they, surprised and ignorant of the numbers of their enemy, or whence they came, made little resistance, and were in a moment smitten and slain. The bones of his father Wahieroa were then eagerly snatched up by him; he hastened with them back to the canoe, embarked on board it, and his warriors at once paddled away, striving to reach his fortified village.

In the morning some of the Ponaturi repaired to their sacred place, and found their priests lying dead there, just as they were slain by Rata. So, without delay, they pursued him. A thousand warriors of their tribe followed after Rata. At length this army reached the fortress of Rata, and an engagement at once took place, in which the tribe of Rata was worsted, and sixty of its warriors slain; at this moment Rata bethought him of the spell he had learnt from the priests, and, immediately repeating the potent incantation Titikura, his slain warriors were by its power once more restored to life; then they rushed again to the combat, and the Ponaturi were slaughtered by Rata and his tribe, a thousand of them—the whole thousand were slain.

Te Rata's task of avenging his father's death being thus ended, his tribe hauled up his large canoe on the shore and roofed it over with thatch to protect it from the sun and weather.

---

1. New Zealand flax.

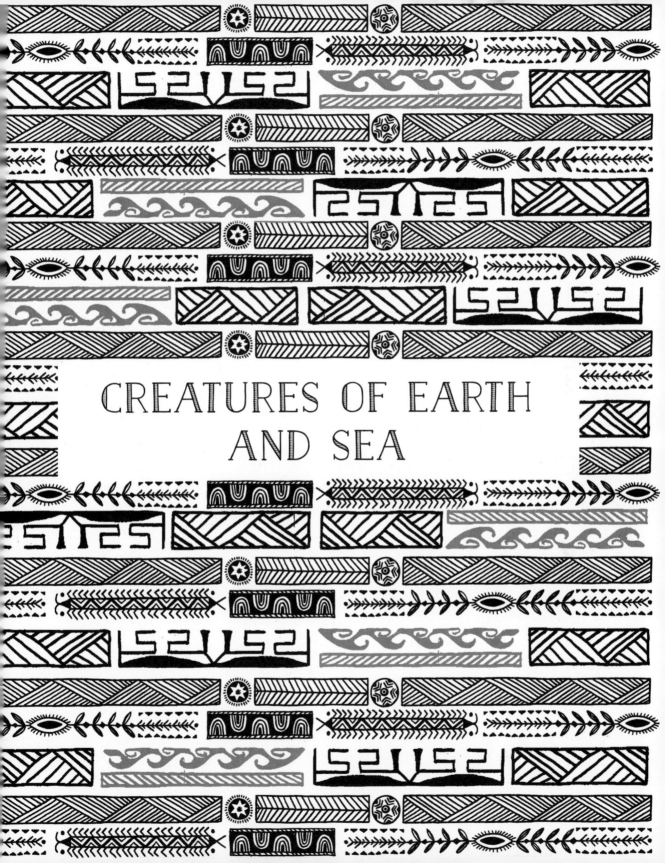

CREATURES OF EARTH AND SEA

THE GREAT BATTLE between the FISH TRIBES and MAN; HOW FISH GAINED THEIR PECULIAR FORMS

New Zealand

There was once a man who was much troubled by the indolence and carelessness of his wife, who, when he returned from sea fishing, was too lazy to carry all the fish home, hence she threw them away, except two or three, which she kept to cook. This went on until the exasperated husband determined to leave her and go in search of a better wife, so he took a firebrand in his hand and went off on his journey. When he entered the forest, he recited certain charms to influence the gods, and then said to the trees of the great forest of Tane—"Should my wife follow me, and ask you any questions, do not tell her aught of me, for she is a bad, lazy woman who wastes the food I procure." To this the trees consented. Then he went on until he came to a stream, where he repeated a charm to influence Tangaroa, then said to the stream—"I am running away from my wife, who is a deceitful person and tiresome. I work to obtain food for us, and she throws it away as food for maggots; hence I go to seek an industrious wife. If my wife follows, and you will know her by her loud voice, do not betray me." And the stream consented to this. So the man fared on until he came to an inland region where dwelt another people, to whom he related his story. So they told him to stay with them and they would protect him in case his enemies attacked him.

On the day on which the husband had set forth, in the evening thereof, his wife went in search of him. When she entered the forest, she asked: "O Trees! Has my husband passed along this path?" But no murmur was heard from the trees, they remained dumb. Then she returned home, for the shades of night were falling. On her return, she enquired of the fire from which her husband had taken a brand: "O Fire! Where is my husband, he who bore away a part of you?" But no word came from the fire. She then saw the gourd vessel used to contain drinking water and said to it: "O Gourd! I see the part of you so often touched by the lips of my husband, and by his breath. Tell me by what path he went when he left me." But no whisper was heard from the gourd. She then turned to the clothing left by her husband and said: "O Garments! Ye that have touched the skin of my husband, and covered him during sleep, thus becoming tapu; reveal to me the way by which my husband departed. But those garments remained silent, and no word was heard. She then addressed his fishing line: "O Line! You who have been handled by the hands of my husband and have heard him repeat his fishing charms; tell me the way by which my husband went." Silent remained that line. She turned to the door of the house, and, placing her hands upon the lintel, spoke: "O Door! Here is the space through which my husband passed in his goings and comings, here the parts his hands touched; tell me by which way he went." But the door stood dumb there, saying no word. Then the woman sat her down and lamented sorely, weeping the whole night, until day came. Then, being athirst, she picked up the water gourd and drank therefrom. Then there came to that gourd a feeling of sympathy, of pity for the woman, because that gourd, of all things, was that which had been closest to her husband, its lips having touched his mouth, even so that gourd felt pity for the weeping woman, and, as she drank, the Gourd spoke, saying: "If you break me, I will conduct you to your husband, I will take you by the way he went, I will convey you over the river he crossed." So off they set together, talking as they went. The woman asked—"When did my husband go?" and the Gourd replied: "He went in the morning."

On arriving at the river, the Gourd said, "Break me again, and I will convey you across the river." She did so, and they crossed over. But on reaching the other side, all became confused, for the Gourd had lost its voice and could no longer speak, having been affected by the charmed water. So the woman had to return to her home, where, after some time, she gave birth to her son.

While her son was yet young, his mother went to Tangaroa (Lord of the Fish) and told her troubles to him. Tangaroa called upon all the fish of Rangiriri to assemble, and they came in their multitudes. Now at that time all fish were alike in form, though differing in size, and all were like the whale, because the whale was the first to be made. Well, Tangaroa told the fish that he wanted them to go and slay a man who had deserted his wife. He formed them into different companies and appointed a commander or chief for each company. These chiefs were named Kumukumu, Parore, Haku, Tamure, Whai, Takeke, Araara, Patiki, and many others, and each company adopted the name of its chief; while Tohora (whale) was appointed supreme chief over all. Tohora compelled his own folk (whales) to keep in rear of the army because, being so large, they would be strong enough to stop a panic and rally the smaller folk.

Then they marched to the place where the fugitive husband was living; for at that time fish had not yet lost their power of living and moving both on land and in the water. It was because fish were descended from lizards that they possessed this power. In making the attack, the company of Kumukumu (the gurnard) led the assault, and many of them were slain, those who escaped being covered with blood, hence the redness of that fish. Also, they moaned in anguish at their loss, hence the moaning of the gurnard when caught. Parore (the black perch) now led his company to the front, where its members got covered with the dried dark blood of the gurnard, hence their colour. Then the company of Haku (the king fish) was beaten by man, as also those of Tamure (snapper), of Whai (stingray), and many others; until Tohora (whale) brought his company up, and before these leviathans the tribe of men gave way and fled.

Then Tangaroa, Lord of the Ocean, made a speech to his army, congratulating the different tribes on the courage they had displayed, and granting each tribe the right to ask for any one boon it might choose at his hands, as a reward for their bravery in action, and in remembrance of their great victory over the man tribe. Also, they might collect and keep the spoils of the battlefield.

So they set about collecting the spoils. Then Whai saw a spear with a double row of barbs on its head, so he asked Tangaroa for a tail like it, and it was given him. Tamure saw a wahaika club and asked that one of his bones should be of a similar form, and Tangaroa granted this request. Patiki (flounder) saw a fly flapper, and wished to be like it in shape, Takeke (garfish) saw a long spear, and asked for a spear on his nose; he got it. Araara (trevally) saw the bloodstained cape of the runaway husband, red spots on a white ground, and desired to resemble it in appearance; and so on, each chief had his wish granted, and he and his folk obtained the form, colour, or other peculiarity desired. This was the origin of the different kinds of fish, and since that time fish have ceased to be all of one shape and colour.

THE SHARK-MAN, NANAUE

Hawai'i

Kamohoalii, the King-shark of Hawai'i and Maui, has several deep sea caves that he uses in turn as his habitat. There are several of these at the bottom of the palisades, extending from Waipio toward Kohala, on the island of Hawai'i. A favorite one was at Koamano, on the mainland, and another was at Maiaukiu, the small islet just abreast of the valley of Waipio. It was the belief of the ancient Hawai'ians that several of these shark gods could assume any shape they chose, the human form even, when occasion demanded.

In the reign of Umi, a beautiful girl, called Kalei, living in Waipio, was very fond of shellfish, and frequently went to Kuiopihi for her favorite article of diet. She generally went in the company of other women, but if the sea was a little rough, and her usual companion was afraid to venture out on the wild and danger-ous beach, she very often went alone rather than go without her favorite seashells.

In those days the Waipio River emptied over a low fall into a basin partly open to the sea; this basin is now completely filled up with rocks from some convulsion of nature, which has happened since then. In this was a deep pool, a favorite bathing-place for all Waipio. The King-shark god, Kamohoalii, used to visit this pool very often to sport in the fresh waters of the Waipio River. Taking into account the many different tales told of the doings of this shark god, he must have had quite an eye for human physical beauty.

Kalei, as was to be expected from a strong, well-formed Hawai'ian girl of those days, was an expert swimmer, a good diver, and noted for the neatness and grace with which she would lelekawa[1] without any splashing of water, which would happen to unskillful divers, from the awkward attitudes they would assume in the act of jumping.

It seems Kamohoalii, the King-shark, had noted the charms of the beautiful Kalei, and his heart, or whatever answers in place of it with fishes, had been captured by them. But he could not expect to make much of an impression on the maiden's susceptibilities *in propria persona*, even though he was perfectly able to take her bodily into his capacious maw; so he must need go courting in a more pleasing way. Assuming the form of a very handsome man, he walked on the beach one rather rough morning, waiting for the girl's appearance.

Now the very wildness of the elements afforded him the chance he desired, as, though Kalei was counted among the most agile and quick of rock-fishers, that morning, when she did come, and alone, as her usual companions were deterred by the rough weather, she made several unsuccessful springs to escape a high threatening wave raised by the god himself; and apparently, if it had not been for the prompt and effective assistance rendered by the handsome stranger, she would have been swept out into the sea.

Thus an acquaintance was established. Kalei met the stranger from time to time, and finally became his wife.

Some little time before she expected to become a mother, her husband, who all this time would only come home at night, told her his true nature, and informing her that he would have to leave her, gave orders in regard to the bringing up of the future child. He particularly cautioned the mother never to let him be fed on animal flesh of any kind, as he would be born with a dual nature, and with a body that he could change at will.

In time Kalei was delivered of a fine healthy boy, apparently the same as any other child, but he had, besides the normal mouth of a human being, a shark's mouth on his back between the shoulder blades. Kalei had told her family of the kind of being her husband was, and they all agreed to keep the matter of the shark-mouth on the child's back a secret, as there was no knowing what fears and jealousies might be excited in the minds of the King or high chiefs by such an abnormal being, and the babe might be killed.

---

1. Jump from the rocks into deep water.

The old grandfather, far from heeding the warning given by Kamohoalii in the matter of animal diet, as soon as the boy, who was called Nanaue, was old enough to come under the taboo in regard to the eating of males and had to take his meals at the mua house with the men of the family, took especial pains to feed him on dog meat and pork. He had a hope that his grandson would grow up to be a great, strong man, and become a famous warrior; and there was no knowing what possibilities lay before a strong, skilful warrior in those days. So he fed the boy with meat, whenever it was obtainable. The boy thrived, grew strong, big, and handsome as a young lama[2] tree.

There was another pool with a small fall of the Waipio River very near the house of Kalei, and the boy very often went into it while his mother watched on the banks. Whenever he got into the water, he would take the form of a shark and would chase and eat the small fish which abounded in the pool. As he grew old enough to understand, his mother took especial pains to impress on him the necessity of concealing his shark nature from other people.

This place was also another favorite bathing-place of the people, but Nanaue, contrary to all the habits of a genuine Hawai'ian, would never go in bathing with the others, but always alone; and when his mother was able, she used to go with him and sit on the banks, holding the kapa scarf, which he always wore to hide the shark-mouth on his back.

When he became a man, his appetite for animal diet, indulged in child-hood, had grown so strong that a human being's ordinary allowance would not suffice for him. The old grandfather had died in the meantime, so that he was dependent on the food supplied by his stepfather and uncles, and they had to expostulate with him on what they called his shark-like voracity. This gave rise to the common native nickname of a manohae[3] for a very gluttonous man, especially in the matter of meat.

Nanaue used to spend a good deal of his time in the two pools, the one inland and the other opening into the sea. The busy-bodies (they had some in those days as well as now) were set to wondering why he always kept a kihei, or mantle, on his shoulders; and for such a handsomely shaped, athletic young

2. *Maba sandwicensis.*

3. Ravenous shark.

man, it was indeed a matter of wonder and speculation, considering the usual attire of the youth of those days. He also kept aloof from all the games and pastimes of the young people, for fear that the wind or some active movement might displace the kapa mantle, and the shark-mouth be exposed to view.

About this time children and eventually grown-up people began to disappear mysteriously.

Nanaue had one good quality that seemed to redeem his apparent unsociability; he was almost always to be seen working in his mother's taro or potato patch when not fishing or bathing. People going to the sea beach would have to pass these potato or taro patches, and it was Nanaue's habit to accost them with the query of where they were going. If they answered, "To bathe in the sea," or, "Fishing," he would answer, "Take care, or you may disappear head and tail." Whenever he so accosted any one it would not be long before some member of the party so addressed would be bitten by a shark.

If it should be a man or woman going to the beach alone, that person would never be seen again, as the shark-man would immediately follow, and watching for a favorable opportunity, jump into the sea. Having previously marked the whereabouts of the person he was after, it was an easy thing for him to approach quite close, and changing into a shark, rush on the unsuspecting person and drag him or her down into the deep, where he would devour his victim at his leisure. This was the danger to humanity which his King-father foresaw when he cautioned the mother of the unborn child about feeding him on animal flesh, as thereby an appetite would be evoked which they had no means of satisfying, and a human being would furnish the most handy meal of the kind that he would desire.

Nanaue had been a man grown some time, when an order was promulgated by Umi, King of Hawai'i, for every man dwelling in Waipio to go to koele work, tilling a large plantation for the King. There were to be certain days in an anahulu[4] to be set aside for this work, when every man, woman, and child had to go and render service, excepting the very old and decrepit, and children in arms.

---

4. Ten days.

The first day everyone went but Nanaue. He kept on working in his mother's vegetable garden to the astonishment of all who saw him. This was reported to the King, and several stalwart men were sent after him. When brought before the King he still wore his kapa kihei, or mantle.

The King asked him why he was not doing koele work with everyone else. Nanaue answered he did not know it was required of him. Umi could not help admiring the bold, free bearing of the handsome man, and noting his splendid physique, thought he would make a good warrior, greatly wanted in those ages, and more especially in the reign of Umi, and simply ordered him to go to work.

Nanaue obeyed and took his place in the field with the others, and proved himself a good worker, but still kept on his kihei, which it would be natural to suppose that he would lay aside as an incumbrance when engaged in hard labor. At last, some of the more venturesome of the younger folks managed to tear his kapa off, as if accidentally, when the shark-mouth on his back was seen by all the people near.

Nanaue was so enraged at the displacement of his kapa and his consequent exposure, that he turned and bit several of the crowd, while the shark-mouth opened and shut with a snap, and a clicking sound was heard such as a shark is supposed to make when baulked by its prey.

The news of the shark-mouth and his characteristic shark-like actions were quickly reported to the King, with the fact of the disappearance of so many people in the vicinity of the pools frequented by Nanaue; and of his pretended warnings to people going to the sea, which were immediately followed by a shark bite or by their being eaten bodily, with every one's surmise and belief that this man was at the bottom of all those disappearances. The King believed it was even so, and ordered a large fire to be lighted, and Nanaue to be thrown in to be burnt alive.

When Nanaue saw what was before him, he called on the shark god, his father, to help him; then, seeming to be endowed with superhuman strength in answer to his prayer, he burst the ropes with which he had been bound in preparation for the burning, and breaking through the throng of Umi's warriors, who attempted to detain him, he ran, followed by the whole multitude, toward the pool that emptied into the sea. When he got to the edge of the rocks bordering the pool, he waited till the foremost persons were within arm's length, when he leaped into the water and immediately turned into a large shark on the surface of the water, in plain view of the people who had arrived, and whose numbers were being continually augmented by more and more arrivals.

He lay on the surface some little time, as if to recover his breath, and then turned over on his back, and raising his head partly out of the water, snapped his teeth at the crowd who, by this time, completely lined the banks, and then, as if in derision or defiance of them, turned and flirted his tail at them and swam out to sea.

The people and chiefs were for killing his mother and relatives for having brought up such a monster. Kalei and her brothers were seized, bound, and dragged before Umi, while the people clamored for their immediate execution, or as some suggested, that they be thrown into the fire lighted for Nanaue.

But Umi was a wise king and would not consent to any such summary proceedings but questioned Kalei in regard to her fearful offspring. The grieved and frightened mother told everything in connection with the paternity and bringing up of the child, and with the warning given by the dread sea-father.

Umi considered that the great sea god Kamohoalii was on the whole a beneficent as well as a powerful one. Should the relatives and mother of that shark god's son be killed, there would then be no possible means of checking the ravages of that son, who might linger around the coast and creeks of the island, taking on human shape at will, for the purpose of travelling inland to any place he liked, and then reassume his fish form and lie in wait in the many deep pools formed by the streams and springs.

Umi, therefore, ordered Kalei and her relatives to be set at liberty, while the priests and shark kahunas were requested to make offerings and invocations to Kamohoalii that his spirit might take possession of one of his hakas,[5] and so express to humanity his desires in regard to his bad son, who had presumed to eat human beings, a practice well known to be contrary to Kamohoalii's design.

---

5. Mediums devoted to his cult.

This was done, whereupon the shark god manifested himself through a haka, and expressed his grief at the action of his wayward son. He told them that the grandfather was to blame for feeding him on animal flesh contrary to his orders, and if it were not for that extenuating circumstance, he would order his son to be killed by his own shark officers; but as it was, he would require of him that he should disappear forever from the shores of Hawai'i. Should Nanaue disregard that order and be seen by any of his father's shark soldiers, he was to be instantly killed.

Then the shark god, who it seems retained an affection for his human wife, exacted a promise that she and her relatives were to be forever free from any persecutions on account of her unnatural son, on pain of the return and freedom from the taboo of that son.

Accordingly, Nanaue left the island of Hawai'i, crossed over to Maui, and landing at Kipahulu, resumed his human shape and went inland. He was seen by the people, and when questioned, told them he was a traveller from Hawai'i, who had landed at Hana and was going around sightseeing. He was so good looking, pleasant, and beguiling in his conversation that people generally liked him. He was taken as aikane by one of the petty chiefs of the place, who gave his own sister for wife to Nanaue. The latter made a stipulation that his sleeping house should be separated from that of his wife, on account of a pretended vow, but really in order that his peculiar second mouth might escape detection.

For a while the charms of the pretty girl who had become his wife seem to have been sufficient to prevent him from trying to eat human beings, but after a while, when the novelty of his position as a husband had worn off, and the desire for human flesh had again become very strong, he resumed the old practice for which he had been driven away from Hawai'i.

He was eventually detected in the very act of pushing a girl into the sea, jumping in after her, then turning into a shark, and commencing to devour her, to the horror of some people who were fishing with hook and rod from some rocks where he had not observed them. These people raised the alarm, and Nanaue, seeing that he was discovered, left for Molokai where he was not known.

He took up his residence on Molokai at Poniuohua, adjoining the ahupuaa of Kainalu, and it was not very long before he was at his old practice of observing and accosting people, giving them his peculiar warning, following them to the sea in his human shape, then seizing one of them as a shark and pulling the unfortunate one to the bottom, where he would devour his victim. In the excitement of such an occurrence, people would fail to notice his absence until he would reappear at some distant point far away from the throng, as if engaged in shrimping or crabbing.

This went on for some time, till the frightened and harassed people in desperation went to consult a shark kahuna, as the ravages of the man-eating shark had put a practical taboo on all kinds of fishing. It was not safe to be anywhere near the sea, even in the shallowest water.

The kahuna told them to lie in wait for Nanaue, and the next time he prophesied that a person would be eaten head and tail, to have some strong men seize him and pull off his kapa mantle, when a shark-mouth would be found on his back. This was done, and the mouth seen, but the shark-man was so strong when they seized him and attempted to bind him, that he broke away from them several times. He was finally overpowered near the seashore and tightly bound. All the people then turned their attention to gathering brush and firewood to burn him, for it was well known that it is only by being totally consumed by fire that a man-shark can be thoroughly destroyed and prevented from taking possession of the body of some harmless fish shark, who would then be incited to do all the pernicious acts of a man-shark.

While he lay there on the low sandy beach, the tide was coming in, and as most of the people were returning with fagots and brush, Nanaue made a supreme effort and rolled over so that his feet touched the water, when he was enabled at once to change into a monster shark. Those who were near him saw it but were not disposed to let him off so easily, and they ran several rows of netting makai, the water being very shallow for quite a distance out. The shark's flippers were all bound by the ropes with which the man Nanaue had been bound, and this with the shallowness of the water prevented him from exerting his great strength to advantage. He did succeed in struggling to the breakers, though momentarily growing weaker from loss of blood, as the people were striking at him with clubs, spears, stone adzes, and anything that would hurt or wound, so as to prevent his escape.

With all that, he would have got clear, if the people had not called to their aid the demigod Unauna, who lived in the mountains of upper Kainalu. It was then a case of Akua vs. Akua, but Unauna was only a young demigod, and not supposed to have acquired his full strength and supernatural powers, while Nanaue was a full-grown man and shark. If it had not been for the latter's being hampered by the cords with which he was bound, the nets in his way, as well as the loss of blood, it is fully believed that he would have got the better of the young local presiding deity; but he was finally conquered and hauled up on the hill slopes of Kainalu to be burnt.

The shallow ravine left by the passage of his immense body over the light yielding soil of the Kainalu Hill slope can be seen to this day, as also a ring or deep groove completely around the top of a tall insulated rock very near the top of Kainalu Hill, around which Unauna had thrown the rope, to assist him in hauling the big shark uphill. The place was ever afterwards called Puumano,[6] and is so known to this day.

Nanaue was so large, that in the attempt to burn him, the blood and water oozing out of his burning body put out the fire several times. Not to be outwitted in that way by the shark son of Kamohoalii, Unauna ordered the people to cut and bring for the purpose of splitting into knives, bamboos from the sacred grove of Kainalu. The shark flesh was then cut into strips, partly dried, and then burnt, but the whole bamboo grove had to be used before the big shark was all cut. The god Mohoalii,[7] father of Unauna, was so angered by the desecration of the grove, or more likely on account of the use to which it was put, that he took away all the edge and sharpness from the bamboos of this grove forever, and to this day they are different from the bamboos of any other place or grove on the islands, in this particular, that a piece of them cannot cut any more than any piece of common wood.

6. Shark Hill.

7. Another form of the name of the god Kamohoalii.

THE STORY of PILI and SINA

Samoa

Loa of Fagaloa was the husband of Sinaletigae who belonged to Afagaloa, a town now extinct between Taga and Salailua in Savai'i. They made their home at Afagaloa and their four children were born here. The names of the children were Sinasamoa (a girl) and Pili, Fuialaeo, and Maomao (boys).

Pili assumed the form of a lizard, and as he grew, he expanded until he filled the house, necessitating the erection of another house for his parents and his brothers and sister. Loa and his wife became so afraid at the size of their son Pili that they fled, taking with them their other three children. They went to Fagaloa, the homeland of Loa. Sinasamoa, the daughter, took away with her the water bottle in which she always carried water to her brother Pili. It was her duty to supply Pili with water and the two brothers supplied him with food. They all still loved Pili, and whenever they sat down to eat, they first of all threw a small portion of food and poured out some water from the water bottle of Pili in remembrance of him.

Pili felt the loss of his parents and brothers and sister and knowing that Fagaloa was the home of his father he assumed the form of a human being again and started out to find the District of Fagaloa, the land of plenty. In due course he arrived and found his sister sitting alone in a fale. She did not know him. On entering the fale, Pili asked as to the whereabouts of his family and was told that they were out working on their plantation. He begged her to go and tell them that a visitor had arrived, but Sina refused to go. Pili then asked for a drink of water from the bottle she had with her. She again refused, stating that the bottle was reserved for her brother Pili. Pili said, "Very well, this place will henceforth be known as Vaitu'u" and the malae is called by this name which means "water reserved or kept here." The place was henceforth looked upon as the ruling town of Fagaloa and still is. Pili asked Sina to state why they had run away from Pili. Sina replied, stating that Pili had grown so big that they were afraid of him and Loa had ordered them to run away and go to his home. It was expected that Pili would follow them when he had reassumed a human form. Pili then said, "I am Pili and I have come to you." The remainder of the family who were in the bush returned and happiness reigned.

Sina became a very beautiful girl, and the word of her loveliness went abroad and was much talked about. The King of Fiji heard of Sina and he paid a visit to Samoa to see her. Loa advised his daughter to become the wife of the King of Fiji, but she would not do so without the consent of her brother Pili. Pili gave his consent because he believed that if children were born as the result of the marriage much power would come to Fagaloa. The ceremony, attended with a great display of the products of the land, took place and was applauded by the Fijians, who acknowledged that their King was fortunate in having found such a beautiful wife.

Preparations for the return journey to Fiji were made and Pili, hearing of them, asked Sina to take him with her because if trouble occurred on the voyage he would be of assistance. Sina did not wish to tell her husband of this arrangement and to hide the presence of Pili she made a small basket into which Pili, who had again assumed the form of a lizard, was hidden.

The canoes were much longer at sea than was usually the case in making a journey to Fiji from Samoa and all the food was consumed. The Fijians blamed their troubles to Sina, who they accused of being possessed of a Devil. When Sina heard the talk of the Fijians she told Pili, who advised her not to bother but to tell the King of Fiji to call in at a small island which lay on the starboard side of the canoe. Here they would find plenty of food in the form of taro, yams, bananas, pigs, fowls, etc. This was done and the King was very surprised. Having replenished their food supplies, the canoes proceeded on their way, but day after day passed without Fiji appearing. Food again ran short, and the people again became anxious. Pili, who was the cause of all this trouble, tapped with his tail on the basket in which he was hidden in order to call Sina's attention. He told Sina to ask the King to call at an island which would be found on the port side of the canoes. They found the island and were again surprised to find a large quantity of food. The Fijians became more than ever suspicious that Sina possessed a Devil, for how otherwise would she know that these islands were in the locality and that there was an abundance of food on them. When Sina heard all this she became afraid and when the King decided to search her to find where the Devil was hidden, she dropped the basket containing Pili into the sea, and this gave rise to the saying "Pili a'au" or "swimming Pili."

Back in Samoa, Loa had a dream which showed that his son Pili had been harshly treated, so he ordered his two sons who had remained with him to launch their canoe and proceed to Fiji to search for Pili. The two brothers started off and after a time came across Pili swimming in the sea. Pili asked them to take him to the island named Pu'agagana and land him and they could then proceed on their way back to Samoa. Tagaloalagi, who was the brother of Loa, predicted what would happen to Pili when he left with Sina. Some time later Tagaloalagi ordered two of his sons to proceed to Fiji to make observations of the group. The sons did as they were ordered and on their way called in at the island of Pu'agagana. As had been predicted by Tagaloalagi, they found Pili sitting on a Pua tree.

When Pili heard that they were going to Fiji he asked to be taken to the home of the King. The elder brother answered, saying that there was not sufficient room in the canoe for another person in addition to which their father had forbidden them to take a third person. Pili said that he did not require a seat as he could be put in the bilge of the canoe and by squeezing he could become very small. He was accordingly taken by the brothers and landed at one end of the town of Tuifiti.

Pili immediately went into the forest and planted various foods. The two brothers assisted him. Beside his Samoan wife, the King of Fiji had a wife from amongst his own people and this wife was much loved by her people. When famine threatened the country, the people brought food for the King and passed it through his Fijian wife, hoping that by so doing he would love only her and hate his Samoan wife, who was not able to present him with food. This so worried Sina that it created in her a continual flow of tears.

Pili, on hearing of Sina's plight, crawled down to the town where the King lived and this action gave rise to the expression "Pili totolo," which means "crawling Pili." He asked Sina to go inland with him and he would show her ways and means of retaining her husband's love. He implored her not to worry as she had brothers who would assist her. Pili told her that all her troubles were due to her weakness in throwing him into the sea. Pili's words pierced her heart and caused the tears to flow faster than ever, and when her husband noticed her plight, he asked the cause. She said that her tears were only for her kind brother Pili in Samoa. She then went with Pili and saw the immense plantation made by Pili and the two brothers for her, the whole plantation being full of food fit for the King.

Pili told Sina that he would create a spring of hot water and also one of cold water so that she could cook and clean her food. A yam would also grow down to her doorstep so that she could reach out and break off pieces to cook. He also advised her that she should always visit him by herself when she wanted anything and she must never tell her husband of his whereabouts. Sina, enriched beyond belief and filled with joy, returned to the village, where she found the springs both hot and cold. These springs still exist in Fiji. Sina also found the ever-creeping yam and this yam was the origin of the saying used by orators "O le Tuli matagau nei le ufi a Sina," which means "searching after the broken end of Sina's yam." The King continued to love Sina and he discarded his Fijian wife. Pili and his two friends returned to Samoa after his sister had given birth to two children, a daughter named Sinavaituu and a son named Latu-Tuifiti.

THE LEGEND of RUANUI

Tahiti

Ruanui was a god who, in order to pass from the invisible world to this earth, found no better way than through the body of a "rori."[1]
He slipped himself into its intestine and arrived safe and sound in this world. He hailed from Faaha in Raiatea, his mother was supposed to be Nioru, and his ancestors were among the shrimp.

But on his way, he lost his hair. And although he had a confident bearing, his skull was elongated, bald, and shiny, so that no woman wanted him. They were all alarmed at the sight of his head.

Nevertheless, by ruse and thanks to the cover of night, he received the favors of a woman named Teahotauniua. He forbade her to touch his head, pretending that it hurt him.

In the morning he rose first and went down to the river to bathe. But soon after, the woman he had slept with arrived as well, with a friend.

Seeing them, Ruanui quickly dove to hide himself under the water until they left. But the river was not deep enough, and his bald scalp remained above the surface.

Teahotauniua said to her friend: "What is that object that we see floating there? Let's take this ball and cut into it to see what it contains."

Ruanui, hearing these words, emerged from the water and ran off, furious.

---

1. Sea cucumber.

He went to complain to his mother about his head being so long and so bald.

She interceded with the gods, who changed the form of his head, but it was still bald.

Then she said to him: "You'll have a head of hair, but be careful to choose well and to reject those that won't suit you."

First of all, the gods gave him a beard[2] of pearl oyster, but he refused it. So they offered him the hair of a rat, but he rejected that too.

Finally, they gave him a beautiful head of thick, black hair and adjusted it upon his head.

He was then so beautiful that all the women loved him, most of all the one he had known. She desired ardently this husband whose beauty she admired.

Her mother counseled her to go to the river where she had seen Ruanui bathing and to get her hands on the first big shrimp she saw in which she could find a resemblance to her lover.

She did so, and lo, the river was swarming with shrimp.

She returned to her mother and said to her: "Never have I seen anything like it; the river is full of shrimp, and they keep arriving without pause."

"Take one," her mother said to her, "lay it out on your knees, and there you'll find Ruanui."

She did so, and she got back her husband.

---

2. Te pito parau.

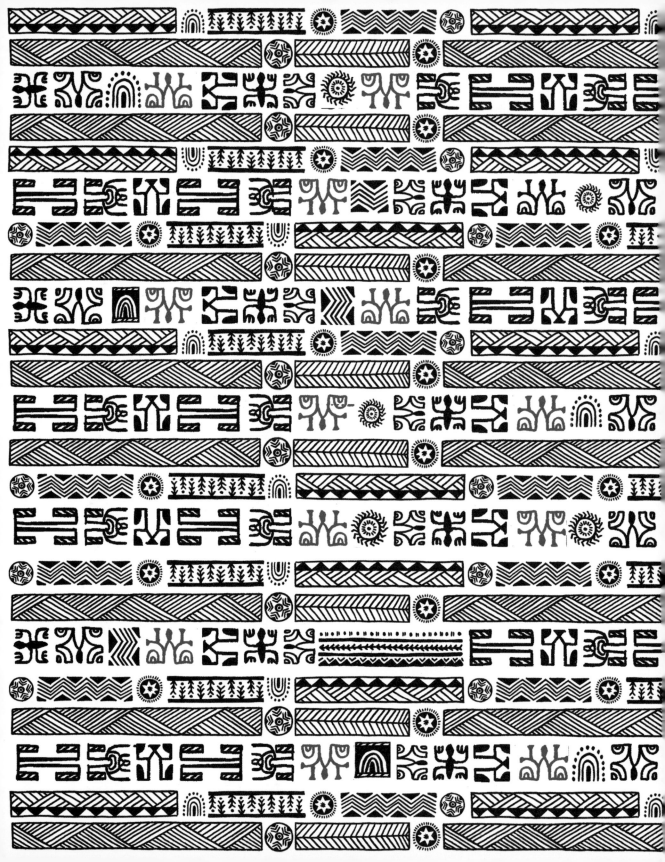

LIFE AND DEATH

AHUULA: A LEGEND of KANIKANIAULA and the FIRST FEATHER CLOAK

Hawai'i

Eleio was a kukini[1] in the service of Kakaalaneo, King of Maui, several runners being always kept by each king or alii of consequence. These kukinis, when sent on any errand, always took a direct line for their destination, climbing hills with the agility of goats, jumping over rocks and streams, and leaping from precipices. They were so fleet of foot that the common illustration of the fact among the natives was the saying that when a kukini was sent on an errand that would ordinarily take a day and a night, fish wrapped in ki leaves,[2] if put on the fire on his starting, would not be cooked sufficiently to be turned before he would be back. Being so serviceable to the aliis, kukinis always enjoyed a high degree of consideration, freedom, and immunity from the strict etiquette and unwritten laws of a Hawai'ian court. There was hardly anything so valuable in their master's possession that they could not have it if they wished.

Eleio was sent to Hana to fetch awa for the King and was expected to be back in time for the King's supper. Kakaalaneo was then living at Lahaina.

---

1. Trained runner.

2. Known as lawalu.

Now, Eleio was not only a kukini, but he was also a kahuna, and had been initiated in the ceremonies and observances by which he was enabled to see spirits or wraiths, and was skilled in medicines, charms, etc., and could return a wandering spirit to its body unless decomposition had set in.

Soon after leaving Olowalu, and as he commenced the ascent of Aalaloloa, he saw a beautiful young woman ahead of him. He naturally hastened his steps, intending to overtake such a charming fellow-traveller; but, do what he would, she kept always just so far ahead of him. Being the fleetest and most renowned kukini of his time, it roused his professional pride to be outrun by a woman, even if only for a short distance; so he was determined to catch her, and he gave himself entirely to that effort. The young woman led him [on] a weary chase over rocks, hills, mountains, deep ravines, precipices, and dark streams, till they came to the Lae[3] of Hanamanuloa at Kahikinui, beyond Kaupo, when he caught her just at the entrance to a puoa. A puoa was a kind of tower, generally of bamboo, with a platform half-way up, on which the dead bodies of persons of distinction belonging to certain families or classes were exposed to the elements.

When Eleio caught the young woman, she turned to him and cried: "Let me live! I am not human, but a spirit, and inside this inclosure is my dwelling."

He answered: "I have been aware for some time of your being a spirit. No human being could have so outrun me."

She then said: "Let us be friends. In yonder house live my parents and relatives. Go to them and ask for a hog, kapas, some fine mats, and a feather cloak. Describe me to them and tell them that I give all those things to you. The feather cloak is unfinished. It is now only a fathom and a half square and was intended to be two fathoms. There are enough feathers and netting in the house to finish it. Tell them to finish it for you." The spirit then disappeared.

Eleio entered the puoa, climbed on to the platform, and saw the dead body of the girl. She was in every way as beautiful as the spirit had appeared to him, and apparently decomposition had not yet set in. He left the puoa and hurried

---

3. Cape.

to the house pointed out by the spirit as that of her friends, and saw a woman wailing, whom, from the resemblance, he at once knew to be the mother of the girl; so he saluted her with an aloha. He then said: "I am a stranger here, but I had a travelling companion who guided me to yonder puoa and then disappeared." At these strange words the woman stopped wailing and called to her husband, to whom she repeated what the stranger had said. The latter then asked: "Does this house belong to you?"

Husband and wife, wondering, answered at once: "It does."

"Then," said Eleio, "my message is to you. My travelling companion has a hog a fathom in length in your care; also a pile of fine kapas of Paiula and others of fine quality; also a pile of mats and an unfinished feather cloak, now a fathom and a half in length, which you are to finish, the materials being in the house. All these things she has given to me and sent me to you for them." Then he began to describe the young woman. Both parents recognized the truthfulness of the description, and willingly agreed to give up the things which their beloved daughter must have herself given away. But when they spoke of killing the hog and making an ahaaina[4] for him, whom they had immediately resolved to adopt as a son, he said: "Wait a little and let me ask: Are all these people I see around this place your friends?"

They both answered: "They are our relatives—uncles, aunts, and cousins to the spirit, who seems to have adopted you either as husband or brother."

"Will they do your bidding in everything?" he asked.

They answered that they could be relied upon. He directed them to build a large lanai, or arbor, to be entirely covered with ferns, ginger, maile, and ieie—the sweet and odorous foliage greens of the islands. An altar was to be erected at one end of the lanai and appropriately decorated. The order was willingly carried out, men, women, and children working with a will, so that the whole structure was finished in a couple of hours.

Eleio now directed the hog to be cooked. He also ordered cooked red and white fish, red, white, and black cocks, and bananas of the lele and maoli

---

4. Feast.

varieties, to be placed on the altar. He ordered all women and children to enter their houses and to assist him with their prayers; all pigs, chickens, and dogs to be tied in dark huts to keep them quiet, and that the most profound silence should be kept. The men at work were asked to remember their gods, and to invoke their assistance for Eleio. He then started for Hana, pulled up a couple of bushes of awa of Kaeleku, famous for its medicinal properties, and was back again before the hog was cooked. The awa was prepared, and when the preparations for the feast were complete and set out, he offered everything to his gods and begged assistance in what he was about to perform.

It seems the spirit of the girl had been lingering near him all the time, seeming to be attached to him, but of course invisible to everyone. When Eleio had finished his invocation he turned and caught the spirit, and, holding his breath and invoking the gods, he hurried to the puoa, followed by the parents, who now began to understand that he was going to try the kapuku[5] on their daughter. Arriving at the puoa, he placed the spirit against the insteps of the girl and pressed it firmly in, meanwhile continuing his invocation. The spirit entered its former tenement kindly enough until it came to the knees, when it refused to go any further, as from there it could perceive that the stomach was beginning to decompose, and it did not want to be exposed to the pollution of decaying matter. But Eleio, by the strength of his prayers, was enabled to push the spirit up past the knees till it came to the thigh bones, when the refractory spirit again refused to proceed. He had to put additional fervor into his prayers to overcome the spirit's resistance, and it proceeded up to the throat, when there was some further check; by this time the father, mother, and male relatives were all grouped around anxiously watching the operation, and they all added the strength of their petitions to those of Eleio, which enabled him to push the spirit past the neck, when the girl gave a sort of crow. There was now every hope of success, and all the company renewed their prayers with redoubled vigor. The spirit made a last feeble resistance at the elbows and wrists, which was triumphantly overborne by the strength of the united

---

5. Or restoration to life of the dead.

prayers. Then it quietly submitted, took complete possession of the body, and the girl came to life. She was submitted to the usual ceremonies of purification by the local priest, after which she was led to the prepared lanai, when kahuna, maid, parents, and relatives had a joyous reunion. Then they feasted on the food prepared for the gods, who were only supposed to absorb the spiritual essence of things, leaving the grosser material parts to their devotees, who, for the time being, are considered their guests.

After the feast the feather cloak, kapas, and fine mats were brought and displayed to Eleio; and the father said to him: "Take the woman thou hast restored and have her for wife and remain here with us; you will be our son and will share equally in the love we have for her."

But our hero, with great self-denial and fidelity, said: "No, I accept her as a charge, but for wife, she is worthy to be that for one higher than I. If you will trust her to me, I will take her to my master, for by her beauty and charms she is worthy to be the queen of our lovely island."

The father answered: "She is yours to do with as you will. It is as if you had created her, for without you, where would she be now? We only ask this, that you always remember that you have parents and relatives here, and a home whenever you choose."

Eleio then asked that the feather cloak be finished for him before he returned to his master. All who could work at feathers set about it at once, including the fair girl restored to life; and he now learned that she was called Kanikaniaula.

When it was completed, he set out on his return to Lahaina accompanied by the girl and taking the feather cloak and the remaining awa he had not used in his incantations. They travelled slowly according to the strength of Kanikaniaula, who now in the body could not equal the speed she had displayed as a spirit.

Arriving at Launiupoko, Eleio turned to her and said: "You wait and hide here in the bushes while I go on alone. If by sundown I do not return, I shall be dead. You know the road by which we came; then return to your people. But if all goes well with me, I shall be back in a little while."

He then went on alone, and when he reached Makila, on the confines of Lahaina, he saw a number of people heating an imu, or underground oven. On perceiving him they started to bind and roast him alive, such being the orders of the King, but he ordered them away with the request, "Let me die at the feet of my master." And thus he passed successfully the imu heated for him.

When he finally stood before Kakaalaneo, the latter said to him: "How is this? Why are you not cooked alive, as I ordered? How came you to pass my lunas?"

The kukini answered: "It was the wish of the slave to die at the feet of his master, if die he must; but if so, it would be an irreparable loss to you, my master, for I have that with me that will cause your name to be renowned and handed down to posterity."

"And what is that?" questioned the King.

Eleio then unrolled his bundle and displayed to the astonished gaze of the King and courtiers the glories of a feather cloak, before then unheard of on the islands. Needless to say, he was immediately pardoned and restored to royal favor, and the awa he had brought from Hana was reserved for the King's special use in his offerings to the gods that evening.

When the King heard the whole story of Eleio's absence, and that the fair original owner was but a short way off, he ordered her to be immediately brought before him that he might express his gratitude for the wonderful garment. When she arrived, he was so struck with her beauty and modest deportment that he asked her to become his Queen. Thus, some of the highest chiefs of the land traced their descent from Kakaalaneo and Kanikaniaula.

The original feather cloak, known as the "Ahu o Kakaalaneo," is said to be in the possession of the Pauahi Bishop Museum. At one time it was used on state occasions as a pa-u, or skirt, by Princess Nahienaena, own sister of the second and third Kamehamehas.

The ahuulas of the ancient Hawai'ians were of fine netting, entirely covered, with feathers woven in. These were either of one color and kind or two or three different colors outlining patterns. The feathers were knotted by twos or threes with twisted strands of the olona, the process being called uo. They were then woven into the foundation netting previously made the exact shape and size wanted. The whole process of feather cloak making was laborious and intricate, and the making of a cloak took a great many years. And as to durability, let the cloak of Kakaalaneo, now several centuries old, attest.

KALELEALUAKA

Hawai'i

PART I

Kaopele was born in Waipio, Hawai'i. When born he did not breathe, and his parents were greatly troubled; but they washed his body clean, and having arrayed it in good clothes, they watched anxiously over the body for several days, and then, concluding it to be dead, placed it in a small cave in the face of the cliff. There the body remained from the summer month of Ikiki[1] to the winter month of Ikua,[2] a period of six months.

At this time they were startled by a violent storm of thunder and lightning, and the rumbling of an earthquake. At the same time appeared the marvellous phenomenon of eight rainbows arching over the mouth of the cave. Above the din of the storm the parents heard the voice of the awakened child calling to them:

> "Let your love rest upon me,
> O my parents, who have thrust me forth,
> Who have left me in the cavernous cliff,
> Who have heartlessly placed me in the
> Cliff frequented by the tropic bird!
> O Waiaalaia, my mother!
> O Waimanu, my father!
> Come and take me!"

---

1. July or August.
2. December or January.

The yearning love of the mother earnestly besought the father to go in quest of the infant; but he protested that search was useless, as the child was long since dead. But, unable longer to endure a woman's teasing, which is the same in all ages, he finally set forth in high dudgeon, vowing that in case of failure he would punish her on his return.

On reaching the place where the babe had been deposited, its body was not to be found. But lifting up his eyes and looking about, he espied the child perched on a tree, braiding a wreath from the scarlet flowers of the lehua.[3] "I have come to take you home with me," said the father. But the infant made no answer. The mother received the child to her arms with demonstrations of the liveliest affection. At her suggestion they named the boy Kaopele, from the name of their goddess, Pele.

Six months after this, on the first day[4] of the new moon, in the month of Ikiki, they returned home from working in the fields and found the child lying without breath, apparently dead. After venting their grief for their darling in loud lamentations, they erected a frame to receive its dead body.

Time healed the wounds of their affection, and after the lapse of six moons they had ceased to mourn, when suddenly they were affrighted by a storm of thunder and lightning, with a quaking of the earth, in the midst of which they distinguished the cry of their child, "Oh, come; come and take me!"

They, overjoyed at this second restoration of their child to them, and deeming it to be a miracle worked by their goddess, made up their minds that if it again fell into a trance they would not be anxious, since their goddess would awake their child and bring it to life again.

But afterward the child informed them of their mistake, saying: "This marvel that you see in me is a trance; when I pass into my deep sleep my spirit at once floats away in the upper air with the goddess, Poliahu. We are a numerous band of spirits, but I excel them in the distance of my flights. In one day I can compass this island of Hawai'i, as well as Maui, Oahu, and Kauai,

---

3. *Metrosideros polymorpha.*
4. Hilo.

and return again. In my flights I have seen that Kauai is the richest of all the islands, for it is well supplied with food and fish, and it is abundantly watered. I intend to remain with you until I am grown; then I shall journey to Kauai and there spend the rest of my life." Thus Kaopele lived with his parents until he was grown, but his habit of trance still clung to him.

Then one day he filled them with grief by saying: "I am going, aloha."

They sealed their love for each other with tears and kisses, and he slept and was gone. He alighted at Kula, on Maui. There he engaged in cultivating food. When his crops were nearly ripe and ready to be eaten, he again fell into his customary deep sleep, and when he awoke he found that the people of the land had eaten up all his crops.

Then he flew away to a place called Kapapakolea, in Moanalua, on Oahu, where he set out a new plantation. Here the same fortune befell him, and his time for sleep came upon him before his crops were fit for eating. When he awoke, his plantation had gone to waste.

Again he moves on, and this time settles in Lihue, Oahu, where for the third time he sets out a plantation of food but is prevented from eating it by another interval of sleep. Awakening, he finds his crops overripe and wasted by neglect and decay.

His restless ambition now carries him to Lahuimalo, still on the island of Oahu, where his industry plants another crop of food. Six months pass, and he is about to eat of the fruits of his labor, when one day, on plunging into the river to bathe, he falls into his customary trance, and his lifeless body is floated by the stream out into the ocean and finally cast up by the waters on the sands of Maeaea, a place in Waialua, Oahu.

At the same time there arrived a man from Kauai in search of a human body to offer as a sacrifice at the temple of Kahikihaunaka at Wailua, on Kauai, and having seen the corpse of Kaopele on the beach, he asks and obtains permission of the feudal lord[5] of Waialua to take it. Thus it happens that Kaopele

---

5. Konohiki.

is taken by canoe to the island of Kauai and placed, along with the corpse of another man, on the altar of the temple at Wailua.

There he lay until the bones of his fellow corpse had begun to fall apart. When six moons had been accomplished, at midnight there came a burst of thunder and an earthquake. Kaopele came to life, descended from the altar, and directed his steps toward a light which he saw shining through some chinks in a neighboring house. He was received by the occupants of the house with that instant and hearty hospitality which marks the Hawai'ian race, and bidden to enter.[6]

Food was set before him, with which he refreshed himself. The old man who seemed to be the head of the household was so much pleased and impressed with the bearing and appearance of our hero that he forthwith sought to secure him to be the husband of his granddaughter, a beautiful girl named Makalani. Without further ado, he persuaded him to be a suitor for the hand of the girl, and while it was yet night, started off to obtain the girl's consent and to bring her back with him.

The young woman was awakened from her slumbers in the night to hear the proposition of her grandfather, who painted to her in glowing colors the manly attractions of her suitor. The suit or found favor in the eyes of the girl's parents and she herself was nothing loath; but with commendable maidenly propriety she insisted that her suitor should be brought and presented to her, and that she should not first seek him.

The sun had hardly begun to lift the dew from the grass when our young hero, accompanied by the two matchmakers, was brought into the presence of his future wife. They found favor in each other's eyes, and an ardent attachment sprang up on the instant. Matters sped apace. A separate house was assigned as the residence of the young couple, and their married life began felicitously.

But the instincts of a farmer were even stronger in the breast of Kaopele than the bonds of matrimony. In the middle of the night he arose, and, leaving the sleeping form of his bride, passed out into the darkness. He went mauka until he came upon an extensive upland plain, where he set to work clearing

---

6. "Mai, komo mai."

and making ready for planting. This done, he collected from various quarters shoots and roots of potato,[7] banana,[8] awa, and other plants, and before day the whole plain was a plantation. After his departure his wife awoke with a start and found her husband was gone. She went into the next house, where her parents were sleeping, and, waking them, made known her loss; but they knew nothing of his whereabouts. Much perplexed, they were still debating the cause of his departure, when he suddenly returned, and to his wife's questioning, answered that he had been at work.

She gently reproved him for interrupting their bridal night with agriculture, and told him there would be time enough for that when they had lived together a while and had completed their honeymoon. "And besides," said she, "if you wish to turn your hand to agriculture, here is the plat of ground at hand in which my father works, and you need not go up to that plain where only wild hogs roam."

To this he replied: "My hand constrains me to plant; I crave work; does idleness bring in anything? There is profit only when a man turns the palm of his hand to the soil: that brings in food for family and friends. If one were indeed the son of a king he could sleep until the sun was high in the heavens, and then rise and find the bundles of cooked food ready for him. But for a plain man, the only thing to do is to cultivate the soil and plant, and when he returns from his work let him light his oven, and when the food is cooked let the husband and the wife crouch about the hearth and eat together."

Again, very early on the following morning, while his wife slept, Kaopele rose, and going to the house of a neighbor, borrowed a fishhook with its tackle. Then, supplying himself with bait, he went a-fishing in the ocean and took an enormous quantity of fish. On his way home he stopped at the house where he had borrowed the tackle and returned it, giving the man also half of the fish. Arrived at home, he threw the load of fish onto the ground with a thud, which waked his wife and parents.

---

7. Kalo.

8. Waoke.

"So you have been a-fishing," said his wife. "Thinking you had again gone to work in the field, I went up there, but you were not there. But what an immense plantation you have set out! Why, the whole plain is covered."

His father-in-law said, "A fine lot of fish, my boy."

Thus went life with them until the crops were ripe, when one day Kaopele said to his wife, who was now evidently with child, "If the child to be born is a boy, name it Kalelealuaka; but if it be a girl, name it as you will, from your side of the family."

From his manner she felt uneasy and suspicious of him, and said, "Alas! do you intend to desert me?"

Then Kaopele explained to his wife that he was not really going to leave her, as men are wont to forsake their wives, but he foresaw that that was soon to happen which was habitual to him, and he felt that on the night of the morrow a deep sleep would fall upon him,[9] which would last for six months. Therefore, she was not to fear.

"Do not cast me out nor bury me in the ground," said he. Then he explained to her how he happened to be taken from Oahu to Kauai and how he came to be her husband, and he commanded her to listen attentively to him and to obey him implicitly. Then they pledged their love to each other, talking and not sleeping all that night.

On the following day all the friends and neighbors assembled, and as they sat about, remarks were made among them in an undertone, like this, "So this is the man who was placed on the altar of the heiau at Wailua." And as evening fell he bade them all aloha, and said that he should be separated from them for six months, but that his body would remain with them if they obeyed his commands. And, having kissed his wife, he fell into the dreamful, sacred sleep of Niolokapu.

On the sixth day the father-in-law said: "Let us bury your husband, lest he stink. I thought it was to be only a natural sleep, but it is ordinary death. Look,

---

9. Puni ka hiamoe.

his body is rigid, his flesh is cold, and he does not breathe; these are the signs of death."

But Makalani protested, "I will not let him be buried; let him lie here, and I will watch over him as he commanded; you also heard his words." But in spite of the wife's earnest protests, the hard-hearted father-in-law gathered strong vines of the koali,[10] tied them about Kaopele's feet, and attaching to them heavy stones, caused his body to be conveyed in a canoe and sunk in the dark waters of the ocean midway between Kauai and Oahu.

Makalani lived in sorrow for her husband until the birth of her child, and as it was a boy, she called his name Kalelealuaka.

PART II

When the child was about two months old the sky became overcast and there came up a mighty storm, with lightning and an earthquake. Kaopele awoke in his dark, watery couch, unbound the cords that held his feet, and by three powerful strokes raised himself to the surface of the water. He looked toward Kauai and Oahu, but love for his wife and child prevailed and drew him to Kauai.

In the darkness of night he stood by his wife's bed and, feeling for her, touched her forehead with his clammy hand. She awoke with a start, and on his making himself known she screamed with fright, "Ghost of Kaopele!" and ran to her parents. Not until a candle was lighted would she believe it to be her husband. The step-parents, in fear and shame at their heartless conduct, fled away, and never returned. From this time forth Kaopele was never again visited by a trance; his virtue had gone out from him to the boy Kalelealuaka.

When Kalelealuaka was ten years old Kaopele began to train the lad in athletic sports and to teach him all the arts of war and combat practised

---

10. Convolvulus.

throughout the islands, until he had attained great proficiency in them. He also taught him the arts of running and jumping, so that he could jump either up or down a high pali, or run, like a waterfowl on the surface of the water. After this, one day Kalelealuaka went over to Wailua, where he witnessed the games of the chiefs. The youth spoke contemptuously of their performances as mere child's play; and when his remark was reported to the King he challenged the young man to meet him in a boxing encounter. When Kalelealuaka came into the presence of the King his royal adversary asked him what wager he brought. As the youth had nothing with him, he seriously proposed that each one should wager his own body against that of the other one. The proposal was readily accepted. The herald sounded the signal of attack, and both contestants rushed at each other. Kalelealuaka warily avoided the attack by the King, and hastened to deliver a blow which left his opponent at his mercy; and thereupon, using his privilege, he robbed the King of his life, and to the astonishment of all, carried away the body to lay as a sacrifice on the altar of the temple, hitherto unconsecrated by human sacrifice, which he and his father Kaopele had recently built in honor of their deity.

After a time there reached the ear of Kalelealuaka a report of the great strength of a certain chief who lived in Hanalei. Accordingly, without saying anything about his intention, he went over to the valley of Hanalei. He found the men engaged in the game of throwing heavy spears at the trunk of a cocoanut tree. As on the previous occasion, he invited a challenge by belittling their exploits, and when challenged by the chief, fearlessly proposed, as a wager, the life of one against the other. This was accepted, and the chief had the first trial. His spear hit the stem of the huge tree and made its lofty crest nod in response to the blow. It was now the turn of Kalelealuaka to hurl the spear. In anticipation of the failure of the youth and his own success, the chief took the precaution to station his guards about Kalelealuaka, to be ready to seize him on the instant. In a tone of command our hero bade the guards fall back, and brandishing his spear, stroked and polished it with his hands from end to end; then he poised and hurled it, and to the astonishment of all, lo! the tree was shivered to pieces. On this the people raised a shout of admiration at the prowess of the youth, and declared he must be the same hero who had slain the chief at Wailua. In this way Kalelealuaka obtained a second royal sacrifice with which to grace the altar of his temple.

One clear, calm evening, as Kalelealuaka looked out to sea, he descried the island of Oahu, which is often clearly visible from Kauai, and asked his father what land that was that stood out against them. Kaopele told the youth it was Oahu; that the cape that swam out into the ocean like a waterfowl was Kaena; that the retreating contour of the coast beyond was Waianae. Thus he described the land to his son. The result was that the adventurous spirit of Kalelealuaka was fired to explore this new island for himself, and he expressed this wish to his father. Everything that Kalelealuaka said or did was good in the eye of his father, Kaopele. Accordingly, he immediately set to work and soon had a canoe completely fitted out, in which Kalelealuaka might start on his travels. Kalelealuaka took with him, as travelling companion, a mere lad named Kaluhe, and embarked in his canoe. With two strokes of the paddle his prow grated on the sands of Waianae.

Before leaving Kauai his father had imparted to Kalelealuaka something of the topography of Oahu, and had described to him the site of his former plantation at Keahumoe. At Waianae the two travellers were treated affably by the people of the district. In reply to the questions put them, they said they were going sight-seeing. As they went along they met a party of boys amusing themselves with darting arrows; one of them asked permission to join their party. This was given, and the three turned inland and journeyed till they reached a plain of soft, whitish rock, where they all refreshed themselves with food. Then they kept on ascending, until Keahumoe lay before them, dripping with hoary moisture from the mist of the mountain, yet as if smiling through its tears. Here were standing bananas with ripened, yellow fruit, upland kalo, and sugar cane, rusty and crooked with age, while the sweet potatoes had crawled out of the earth and were cracked and dry. It was the very place where Kaopele, the father of Kalelealuaka, had years before set out the plants from which these were descended.

"This is our food, and a good place, perhaps, for us to settle down," said Kalelealuaka; "but before we make up our minds to stay here let me dart an arrow; and if it drops soon we shall stay, but if it flies afar we shall not tarry here." Kalelealuaka darted his arrow, while his companions looked on intently. The arrow flew along, passing over many a hill and valley, and finally rested beyond Kekuapoi, while they followed the direction of its wonderful flight. Kalelealuaka sent his companions on to find the arrow, telling them at the same time to go to the villages and get some awa roots for drink, while he would remain there and put up a shelter for them.

On their way the two companions of Kalelealuaka encountered a number of women washing kalo in a stream, and on asking them if they had seen their arrow flying that way they received an impertinent answer; whereupon they called out the name of the arrow, "Pua-ne, Pua-ne," and it came to their hands at once. At this the women ran away, frightened at the marvel.

The two boys then set to gathering awa roots, as they had been bidden. Seeing them picking up worthless fragments, a kind-hearted old man, who turned out to be the konohiki of the land, sent by his servants an abundance of good food to Kalelealuaka.

On their return the boys found, to their astonishment, that during their absence Kalelealuaka had put up a fine, large house, which was all complete but the mats to cover the floors. The kind-hearted konohiki remarked this, and immediately sent his servants to fetch mats for the floors and sets of kapa for bedding, adding the command, "And with them bring along some malos."[11] Soon all their wants were supplied, and the three youths were set up in housekeeping. To these services the konohiki, through his attendants, added still others; some chewed and strained the awa, while others cooked and spread for them a bountiful repast. The three youths ate and drank, and under the drowsy influence of the awa they slept until the little birds that peopled the wilderness about them waked them with their morning songs; then they roused and found the sun already climbing the heavens.

---

11. Girdles used by the males.

Now, Kalelealuaka called to his comrades, and said, "Rouse up and let us go to cultivating." To this they agreed, and each one set to work in his own way, working his own piece of ground. The ground prepared by Kalelealuaka was a strip of great length, reaching from the mountain down toward the ocean. This he cleared and planted the same day. His two companions, however, spent several days in clearing their ground, and then several days more in planting it. While these youths occupied their mountain home, the people of that region were well supplied with food. The only lack of Kalelealuaka and his comrades was animal food,[12] but they supplied its place as well as they could with such herbs as the tender leaves of the popolo, which they cooked like spinach, and with inamona made from the roasted nuts of the kukui tree.[13]

One day, as they were eking out their frugal meal with a mess of popolo cooked by the lad from Waianae, Kalelealuaka was greatly disgusted at seeing a worm in that portion that the youth was eating, and thereupon nicknamed him Keinohoomanawanui.[14] The name ever after stuck to him. This same fellow had the misfortune, one evening, to injure one of his eyes by the explosion of a kukui nut which he was roasting on the fire. As a result, that member was afflicted with soreness, and finally became blinded. But their life agreed with them, and the youths throve and increased in stature, and grew to be stout and lusty young men.

Now, it happened that ever since their stay at their mountain house, Lelepua,[15] they had kept a torch burning all night, which was seen by Kakuhihewa, the King of Oahu, and had caused him uneasiness.

One fine evening, when they had eaten their fill and had gone to bed, Kalelealuaka called to Keinohoomanawanui and said, "Halloo there! Are you asleep?"

---

12. Literally, fish.

13. *Aleurites molluccana.*

14. Sloven, or more literally, the persistently unclean.

15. Arrow flight.

And he replied, "No; have I drunk awa? I am restless. My eyes will not close."

"Well," said Kalelealuaka, "when you are restless at night, what does your mind find to do?"

"Nothing," said the Sloven.

"I find something to think about," said Kalelealuaka.

"What is that?" said the Sloven.

"Let us wish,"[16] said Kalelealuaka.

"What shall we wish?" said the Sloven.

"Whatever our hearts most earnestly desire," said Kalelealuaka. Thereupon they both wished. The Sloven, in accordance with his nature, wished for things to eat—the eels, from the fish-pond of Hanaloa (in the district of Ewa), to be cooked in an oven together with sweet potatoes, and a bowl of awa.

"Pshaw, what a beggarly wish!" said Kalelealuaka. "I thought you had a real wish. I have a genuine wish. Listen: The beautiful daughters of Kakuhihewa to be my wives; his fatted pigs and dogs to be baked for us; his choice kalo, sugar cane, and bananas to be served up for us; that Kakuhihewa himself send and get timber and build a house for us; that he pull the famous awa of Kahauone; that the King send and fetch us to him; that he chew the awa for us in his own mouth, strain and pour it for us, and give us to drink until we are happy, and then take us to our house."

Trembling with fear at the audacious ambition of his concupiscent companion, the Sloven replied, "If your wish should come to the ears of the King, we shall die; indeed, we should die."

In truth, as they were talking together and uttering their wishes, Kakuhihewa had arrived, and was all the time listening to their conversation from the outside of their house. When the King had heard their conversation, he thrust his spear into the ground outside the inclosure about Kalelealuaka's house, and by the spear placed his stone weapon,[17] and immediately returned to

---

16. Kuko, literally, to lust.

17. Pahoa.

his residence at Puuloa. Upon his arrival at home that night King Kakuhihewa commanded his stewards to prepare a feast, and then summoned his chiefs and table companions and said, "Let us sup." When all was ready and they had seated themselves, the King said, "Shall we eat, or shall we talk?"

One of them replied: "If it please the King, perhaps it were better for him to speak first; it may be what he has to say touches a matter of life and death; therefore, let him speak and we will listen."

Then Kakuhihewa told them the whole story of the light seen in the mountains, and of the wishes of Kalelealuaka and the Sloven.

Then up spoke the soldiers and said: "Death! This man is worthy to be put to death; but as for the other one, let him live."

"Hold," said the King, "not so fast! Before condemning him to death, I will call together the wise men, priests, wizards, and soothsayers; perchance they will find that this is the man to overcome Kualii in battle." Thereupon all the wise men, priests, wizards, and soothsayers were immediately summoned, and after the King had explained the whole story to them they agreed with the opinion of the soldiers. Again the King interposed delay, and said, "Wait until my wise kahuna Napuaikamao comes; if his opinion agrees with yours, then, indeed, let the man be put to death; but if he is wiser than you, the man shall live. But you will have eaten this food in vain."

So the King sent one of his fleetest runners to go and fetch Napuaikamao. To him the King said, "I have sent for you to decide what is just and right in the case of these two men who live up in the region of Waipio." Then he went on to state the whole case to this wise man.

"In regard to Keinohoomanawanui's wish," said the wise man, "that is an innocent wish, but it is profitless and will bring no blessing." At the narration of Kalelealuaka's wish he inclined his head, as if in thought; then lifting his head, he looked at the King and said: "O King, as for this man's wish, it is an ambition which will bring victory to the government. Now, then, send all your people and fetch house-timber and awa."

As soon as the wise man had given this opinion, the King commanded his chief marshal, Maliuhaaino, to set everyone to work to carry out the directions of this counsellor. This was done, and before break of day every man, woman, and child in the district of Ewa, a great multitude, was on the move.

Now, when the Sloven awoke in the morning and went out of doors, he found the stone hatchet[18] of the King, with his spear, standing outside of the house. On seeing this he rushed back into the house and exclaimed to his comrades, "Alas! our wishes have been overheard by the King; here are his hatchet and his spear. I said that if the King heard us we should die, and he has indeed heard us. But yours was the fatal ambition; mine was only an innocent wish."

Even while they were talking, the babble of the multitude drew near, and the Sloven exclaimed, "Our death approaches!"

Kalelealuaka replied, "That is not for our death; it is the people coming to get timber for our houses." But the fear of the Sloven would not be quieted.

The multitude pressed on, and by the time the last of them had reached the mountain the foremost had returned to the seacoast and had begun to prepare the foundations for the houses, to dig the holes for the posts, to bind on the rafters and the small poles on which they tied the thatch, until the houses were done.

Meantime, some were busy baking the pigs and the poi-fed dogs in ovens; some in bringing the eels of Kanaloa and cooking them with potatoes in an oven by themselves.

The houses are completed, everything is ready, the grand marshal, Maliuhaaino, has just arrived in front of the house of the ambitious youth Kalelealuaka, and calls out, "Keinohoomanawanui, come out!" and he comes out, trembling. "Kalelealuaka, come out!" and he first sends out the boy Kaluhe and then comes forth himself and stands outside, a splendid youth. The marshal stands gazing at him in bewilderment and admiration. When he has regained his equanimity he says to him, "Mount on my back and let us go down."

"No," said Kalelealuaka, "I will go by myself, and do you walk ahead. I will follow after; but do not look behind you, lest you die."

---

18. Pahoa.

As soon as they had started down, Kalelealuaka was transported to Kuaikua, in Helemano. There he plunged into the water and bathed all over; this done, he called on his ancestral shades,[19] who came and performed on him the rite of circumcision while lightning flashed, thunder sounded, and the earth quaked.

Kaopele, on Kauai, heard the commotion and exclaimed, "Ah! My son has received the purifying rite—the offspring of the gods goes to meet the sovereign of the land."[20]

Meanwhile, the party led by Maliuhaaino was moving slowly down toward the coast, because the marshal himself was lame. Returning from his purification, Kalelealuaka alighted just to the rear of the party, who had not noticed his absence, and becoming impatient at the tedious slowness of the journey—for the day was waning, and the declining sun was already standing over a peak of the Waianae Mountains called Puukuua—this marvellous fellow caught up the lame marshal in one hand and his two comrades in the other, and, flying with them, set them down at Puuloa. But the great marvel was that they knew nothing about being transported, yet they had been carried and set down as from a sheet.

On their arrival at the coast all was ready, and the people were waiting for them. A voice called out, "Here is your house, Keinohoomanawanui!" and the Sloven entered with alacrity and found bundles of his wished-for eels and potatoes already cooked and awaiting his disposal.

But Kalelealuaka proudly declined to enter the house prepared for himself when the invitation came to him, "Come in! This is your house," all because his little friend Kaluhe, whose eyes had often been filled with smoke while cooking luau and roasting kukui nuts for him, had not been included in the invitation, and he saw that no provision had been made for him. When this was satisfactorily arranged Kalelealuaka and his little friend entered and sat down to eat. The King, with his own hand, poured out awa for Kalelealuaka,

---

19. Aumakua.

20. Alii aimoku.

brought him a gourd of water to rinse his mouth, offered him food, and waited upon him till he had supplied all his wants.

Now, when Kalelealuaka had well drunken, and was beginning to feel drowsy from the awa, the lame marshal came in and led him to the two daughters of Kakuhihewa, and from that time these two lovely girls were his wives.

PART III

Thus they lived for perhaps thirty days,[21] when a messenger arrived, announcing that Kualii was making war at Moanalua. The soldiers of Kakuhihewa quickly made themselves ready, and among them Keinohoomanawanui went out to battle. The lame marshal had started for the scene the night before.

On the morning of the day of battle, Kalelealuaka said to his wives that he had a great hankering for some shrimps and moss, which must be gathered in a particular way, and that nothing else would please his appetite. Thereupon, they dutifully set out to obtain these things for him. As soon as they had gone from the house Kalelealuaka flew to Waianae and arrayed himself with wreaths of the fine-leaved maile,[22] which is peculiar to that region. Thence he flew to Napeha, where the lame marshal, Maliuhaaino, was painfully climbing the hill on his way to battle. Kalelealuaka cheerily greeted him, and the following dialogue occurred:

K. "Whither are you trudging, Maliuhaaino?"

M. "What! Don't you know about the war?"

K. "Let me carry you."

M. "How fast you travel! Where are you from?"

---

21. He mau anahulu.

22. *Maile laulii.*

K. "From Waianae."

M. "So I see from your wreaths. Yes, carry me, and Waianae shall be yours."

At the word Kalelealuaka picked up Maliuhaaino and set him down on an eminence mauka of the battlefield, saying, "Remain you here and watch me. If I am killed in the fight, you return by the same way we came and report to the King."

Kalelealuaka then addressed himself to the battle, but before attacking the enemy he revenged himself on those who had mocked and jeered at him for not joining the forces of Kakuhihewa. This done, he turned his hand against the enemy, who at the time were advancing and inflicting severe loss in the King's army.

To what shall we compare the prowess of our hero? A man was plucked and torn in his hand as if he were but a leaf. The commotion in the ranks of the enemy was as when a powerful waterfowl lashes the water with his wings.[23] Kalelealuaka moved forward in his work of destruction until he had slain the captain who stood beside the rebel chief, Kualii. From the fallen captain he took his feather cloak and helmet and cut off his right ear and the little finger of his right hand. Thus ended the slaughter that day.

The enthusiasm of Maliuhaaino was roused to the highest pitch on witnessing the achievements of Kalelealuaka, and he determined to return and report that he had never seen his equal on the battlefield.

Kalelealuaka returned to Puuloa and hid the feather cloak and helmet under the mats of his bed, and having fastened the dead captain's ear and little finger to the side of the house, lay down and slept.

After a while, when the two women, his wives, returned with the moss and shrimps, he complained that the moss was not gathered as he had directed, and that they had been gone such a long time that his appetite had entirely left him, and he would not eat of what they had brought. At this the elder sister said nothing, but the younger one muttered a few words to herself; and as they were all very tired they soon went to sleep.

---

23. O haehae ka manu, Ke ale nei ka wai.

They had slept a long while when the tramp of the soldiers of Kakuhihewa was heard, returning from the battle. The King immediately asked how the battle had gone. The soldiers answered that the battle had gone well, but that Keinohoomanawanui alone had greatly distinguished himself. To this the King replied he did not believe that the Sloven was a great warrior, but when Maliuhaaino returned he would learn the truth.

About midnight the footsteps of the lame marshal were heard outside of the King's house. Kakuhihewa called to him, "Come, how went the battle?"

"Can't you have patience and let me take breath?" said the marshal. Then when he had rested himself he answered, "They fought, but there was one man who excelled all the warriors in the land. He was from Waianae. I gave Waianae to him as a reward for carrying me."

"It shall be his," said the King.

"He tore a man to pieces," said Maliuhaaino, "as he would tear a banana-leaf. The champion of Kualii's army he killed and plundered him of his feather cloak and helmet."

"The soldiers say that Keinohoomanawanui was the hero of the day," said the King.

"What!" said Maliuhaaino. "He did nothing. He merely strutted about. But this man—I never saw his equal; he had no spear, his only weapons were his hands; if a spear was hurled at him, he warded it off with his hair. His hair and features, by the way, greatly resemble those of your son-in-law."

Thus they conversed till daybreak.

After a few days, again came a messenger announcing that the rebel Kualii was making war on the plains of Kulaokahua. On hearing this Kakuhihewa immediately collected his soldiers. As usual, the lame marshal set out in advance the evening before the battle.

In the morning, after the army had gone, Kalelealuaka said to his wives, "I am thirsting for some water taken with the snout of the calabash held downward. I shall not relish it if it is taken with the snout turned up." Now, Kalelealuaka knew that they could not fill the calabash if held this way, but he resorted to this artifice to prevent the two young women from knowing of his miraculous flight to the battle. As soon as the young women had got out of sight he hastened to Waialua and arrayed himself in the rough and shaggy wreaths of uki from the lagoons of Ukoa and of hinahina from Kealia. Thus arrayed, he alighted behind the lame marshal as he climbed the hill at Napeha, slapped him on the back, exchanged greetings with him, and received a compliment on his speed; and when asked whence he came, he answered from Waialua. The shrewd, observant marshal recognized the wreaths as being those of Waialua, but he did not recognize the man, for the wreaths with which Kalelealuaka had decorated himself were of such a color—brownish grey—as to give him the appearance of a man of middle age. He lifted Maliuhaaino as before, and set him down on the brow of Puowaina,[24] and received from the grateful man, as a reward for his service, all the land of Waialua for his own.

This done, Kalelealuaka repeated the performances of the previous battle. The enemy melted away before him, whichever way he turned. He stayed his hand only when he had slain the captain of the host and stripped him of his feather cloak and helmet, taking also his right ear and little finger. The speed with which Kalelealuaka returned to his home at Puuloa was like the flight of a bird. The spoils and trophies of this battle he disposed of as before.

The two young women, Kalelealuaka's wives, turned the nozzle of the water-gourd downward, as they were bidden, and continued to press it into the water, in the vain hope that it might rise and fill their container, until the noonday sun began to pour his rays directly upon their heads; but no water entered their calabash. Then the younger sister proposed to the elder to fill the calabash in the usual way, saying that Kalelealuaka would not know the difference. This they did and returned home.

Kalelealuaka would not drink of the water, declaring that it had been dipped up. At this the younger wife laughed furtively; the elder broke forth and said: "It is due to the slowness of the way you told us to employ in getting the water. We are not accustomed to the menial office of fetching water; our father treated us delicately, and a man always fetched water for us, and we always

---

24. Punch Bowl Hill.

used to see him pour the water into the gourd with the nozzle turned up, but you trickily ordered us to turn the nozzle down. Your exactions are heartless."

Thus the women kept complaining until, by and by, the tramp of the returning soldiers was heard, who were boasting of the great deeds of Keinohoomanawanui. The King, however, said: "I do not believe a word of your talk; when my marshal comes he will tell me the truth. I do not believe that Keinohoomanawanui is an athlete. Such is the opinion I have formed of him. But there is a powerful man, Kalelealuaka—if he were to go into battle I am confident he would perform wonders. Such is the opinion I have formed of him, after careful study."

So the King waited for the return of Maliuhaaino until night, and all night until nearly dawn. When finally the lame marshal arrived, the King prudently abstained from questioning him until he had rested a while and taken breath; then he obtained from him the whole story of this new hero from Waialua, whose name he did not know, but who, he declared, resembled the King's son-in-law, Kalelealuaka.

Again, on a certain day, came the report of an attack by Kualii at Kulaokahua, and the battle was to be on the morrow. Maliuhaaino, as usual, started off the evening before. In the morning, Kalelealuaka called to his wives, and said: "Where are you? Wake up. I wish you to bake a fowl for me. Do it thus: Pluck it; do not cut it open, but remove the inwards through the opening behind; then stuff it with luau from the same end, and bake it; by no means cut it open, lest you spoil the taste of it."

As soon as they had left the house, he flew to Kahuku and adorned his neck with wreaths of the pandanus fruit and his head with the flowers of the sugar cane, thus entirely changing his appearance and making him look like a grey-haired old man. As on previous days, he paused behind Maliuhaaino and greeted him with a friendly slap on the back. Then he kindly lifted the lame man and set him down at Puowaina. In return for this act of kindness the marshal gave him the district of Koolau.

In this battle he first slew those soldiers in Kakuhihewa's army who had spoken ill of him. Then he turned his hand against the warriors of Kualii, smiting them as with the stroke of lightning, and displaying miraculous powers. When he had reached the captain of Kualii's force, he killed him and despoiled his body of his feather cloak and helmet, taking also a little finger and toe. With these he flew to the marshal, whom he lifted and bore in his flight as far as Waipio, and there dropped him at a point just below where the water bursts forth at Waipahu.

Arrived at his house, Kalelealuaka, after disposing of his spoils, lay down and slept. After he had slept several hours, his wives came along in none too pleased a mood and awoke him, saying his meat was cooked. Kalelealuaka merely answered that it was so late his appetite had gone, and he did not care to eat.

At this slight his wives said: "Well, now, do you think we are accustomed to work? We ought to live without work, like a king's daughters, and when the men have prepared the food then we should go and eat it."

The women were still muttering over their grievance, when along came the soldiers, boasting of the powers of Keinohoomanawanui, and as they passed Kalelealuaka's door they said it were well if the two wives of this fellow, who lounges at home in time of war, were given to such a brave and noble warrior as Keinohoomanawanui.

The sun was just sinking below the ocean when the footsteps of Maliuhaaino were heard at the King's door, which he entered, sitting down within. After a short time the King asked him about the battle. "The valor and prowess of this third man were even greater than those of the previous ones; yet all three resemble each other. This day, however, he first avenged himself by slaying those who had spoken ill of him. He killed the captain of Kualii's army and took his feather cloak and helmet. On my return he lifted me as far as Waipahu."

In a few days again came a report that Kualii had an army at a place called Kahapaakai, in Nuuanu. Maliuhaaino immediately marshalled his forces and started for the scene of battle the same evening.

Early the next morning Kalelealuaka awakened his wives, and said to them: "Let us breakfast, but do you two eat quietly in your own house, and

I in my house with the dogs; and do not come until I call you." So they did, and the two women went and breakfasted by themselves. At his own house Kalelealuaka ordered Kaluhe to stir up the dogs and keep them barking until his return. Then he sprang away and lighted at Kapakakolea, where he overtook Maliuhaaino, whom, after the usual interchange of greetings, he lifted, and set down at a place called Waolani.

On this day his first action was to smite and slay those who had reviled him at his own door. That done, he made a great slaughter among the soldiers of Kualii; then, turning, he seized Keinohoomanawanui, threw him down and asked him how he became blinded in one eye.

"It was lost," said the Sloven, "from the thrust of a spear, in a combat with Olopana."

"Yes, to be sure," said Kalelealuaka, "while you and I were living together at Wailuku, you being on one side of the stream and I on the other, a kukui nut burst in the fire, and that was the spear that put out your eye."

When the Sloven heard this, he hung his head. Then Kalelealuaka seized him to put him to death, when the spear of the Sloven pierced the fleshy part of Kalelealuaka's left arm, and in plucking it out the spearhead remained in the wound.

Kalelealuaka killed Keinohoomanawanui and beheaded him, and, running to the marshal, laid the trophy at his feet with the words: "I present you, Maliuhaaino, with the head of Keinohoomanawanui." This done, he returned to the battle, and went on slaying until he had advanced to the captain of Kualii's forces, whom he killed and spoiled of his feather cloak and helmet.

When Kualii saw that his chief captain, the bulwark of his power, was slain, he retreated and fled up Nuuanu Valley, pursued by Kalelealuaka, who overtook him at the head of the valley. Here Kualii surrendered himself, saying: "Spare my life. The land shall all go to Kakuhihewa, and I will dwell on it as a loyal subject under him and create no disturbance as long as I live."

To this the hero replied: "Well said! I spare your life on these terms. But if you at any time foment a rebellion, I will take your life! So, then, return, and live quietly at home and do not stir up any war in Koolau." Thus warned, Kualii set out to return to the "deep blue palis of Koolau."

While the lame marshal was trudging homeward, bearing the head of the Sloven, Kalelealuaka alighted from his flight at his house, and having disposed in his usual manner of his spoils, immediately called to his wives to rejoin him at his own house.

The next morning, after the sun was warm, Maliuhaaino arrived at the house of the King in a state of great excitement and was immediately questioned by him as to the issue of the battle. "The battle was altogether successful," said the marshal, "but Keinohoomanawanui was killed. I brought his head along with me and placed it on the altar mauka of Kalawao. But I would advise you to send at once your fleetest runners through Kona and Koolau, commanding everybody to assemble in one place, that I may review them and pick out and vaunt as the bravest that one whom I shall recognize by certain marks—for I have noted him well: he is wounded in the left arm."

Now, Kakuhihewa's two swiftest runners[25] were Keakealani and Kuhele-moana. They were so fleet that they could compass Oahu six times in a fore-noon, or twelve times in a whole day. These two were sent to call together all the men of the King's domain. The men of Waianae came that same day and stood in review on the sandy plains of Puuloa. But among them all was not one who bore the marks sought for. Then came the men of Kona, of Waialua, and of Koolau, but the man was not found.

Then the lame marshal came and stood before the King and said: "Your bones shall rest in peace, Kalani. You had better send now and summon your son-in-law to come and stand before me; for he is the man." Then Kakuhihewa arose and went himself to the house of his son-in-law, and called to his daughters that he had come to get their husband to go and stand before Maliuhaaino.

Then Kalelealuaka lifted up the mats of his bed and took out the feather cloaks and the helmets and arrayed his two wives, and Kaluhe, and himself. Putting them in line, he stationed the elder of his wives first, next to her the

---

25. Kukini.

younger, and third Kaluhe, and placing himself at the rear of the file, he gave the order to march, and thus accompanied he went forth to obey the King's command.

The lame marshal saw them coming, and in ecstasy he prostrated himself and rolled over in the dust. "The feather cloak and the helmet on your elder daughter are the ones taken from the captain of Kualii's army in the first day's fight; those on your second daughter from the captain of the second day's fight; while those on Kalelealuaka himself are from the captain killed in the battle on the fourth day. You will live, but perhaps I shall die, since he is weary of carrying me."

The lame marshal went on praising and eulogizing Kalelealuaka as he drew near. Then addressing the hero, he said: "I recognize you, having met you before. Now show your left arm to the King and to this whole assembly, that they may see where you were wounded by the spear."

Then Kalelealuaka bared his left arm and displayed his wound to the astonished multitude. Thereupon Kakuhihewa said: "Kalelealuaka and my daughters, do you take charge of the kingdom, and I will pass into the ranks of the common people under you."

After this a new arrangement of the lands was made, and the country had peace until the death of Kakuhihewa; Kalelealuaka also lived peacefully until death took him.

THE ORIGIN of the NAME
of PUNAAUIA

Tahiti

A young man from Fautaua named Temuri, handsome in stature and visage but of base extraction, was going to fish for mullet near Faaa when he met on the beach the beautiful princess Pereitai, daughter of the noble house of Maheanuu. They fell in love with each other and met several times. And at last, the young princess declared to her parents that she wanted no other husband than the handsome Temuri. Naturally, the parents couldn't consent to a misalliance of this sort. Having learned that the two lovers had resolved to run away together to the city of refuge, Papenoo, they dispatched to the rendezvous point a priest, who knocked Temuri over the head with a club and buried him properly at the royal marae of Ahurai in Fataa.

The young Pereitai was inconsolable over the death of Temuri. She cried many days and many nights, and her health declined. To distract her from her grief, her parents sent her on a journey to the Iles-Sous-le-Vent with her younger brother, Matairuapuna.

In Raiatea, where the royal family of Tamatoa received them with many honors, the young chief Teraimarama asked for Pereitai's hand in marriage. She accepted in order to please her parents, although she had not yet forgotten Temuri. The marriage was celebrated with great pomp, and after a year, a little girl was born, as pretty as her mother.

But a few months later, over the trivial matter of a tapa, Pereitai felt humiliated by the women of Raiatea. She fled to the valley of Faaroa and sat herself down to cry on a great stone, in the place called Teoraaotaha. Today, one can still see this stone speckled with white spots, the traces of Pereitai's tears.

Her brother searched for her and found her there. But when she caught sight of him, she plunged into a deep hole at the bottom of the river. He dove in after her, and both of them descended through a dark passage dug out of the rock and arrived in Po, the realm of shadows, where souls lived. The siblings were well received by their ancestors and remained there one year, and Pereitai forgot her grief.

In this dwelling place of the dead, there were immense ocean conch shells, from which the spirits drew harmonious sounds. Even now, on calm nights, when the fishermen of Punaauia pass close to a great fissure in the reef called Toatemiro, they sometimes hear the music of the spirits.

One of these conch shells was given to the younger brother of Pereitai, and he quickly learned to play it skillfully.

They remained there one year, and then they were told that it was time to return to the realm of the living, and they were shown a long tunnel that led them all the way to Tahiti, to the district of Punaauia, which at the time was called Manotahi. They emerged in a cave at the edge of the sea, and immediately, the young man began playing his trumpet.

All the inhabitants came running, recognized the siblings, and welcomed them joyfully.

Matairuapuna gave his conch as a gift to the great chief Pohuetea, who, to commemorate this marvellous episode, changed the name of the district from Manotahi to Punaauia, "the trumpet is mine."

KAALA, the FLOWER of LANAI:
A STORY of the SPOUTING CAVE
of PALIKAHOLO

Hawai'i

PART I

Beneath one of the boldest of the rocky bluffs against which dash the breakers of Kaumalapau Bay, on the little island of Lanai, is the Puhio-Kaala, or "Spouting Cave of Kaala." The only entrance to it is through the vortex of a whirlpool, which marks the place where, at intervals, the receding waters rise in a column of foam above the surface. Within, the floor of the cave gradually rises from the opening beneath the waters until a landing is reached above the level of the tides, and to the right and left, farther than the eye can penetrate by the dim light struggling through the surging waves, stretch dank and shelly shores, where crabs, polypii, stingrays, and other noisome creatures of the deep find protection against their larger enemies.

This cavern was once a favorite resort of Mooalii, the great lizard-god; but as the emissaries of Ukanipo, the shark-god, annoyed him greatly and threatened to imprison him within it by piling a mountain of rocks against the opening, he abandoned it and found a home in a cave near Kaulapapa, in the neighboring island of Molokai, where many rude temples were erected to him by the fishermen.

Before the days of Kamehameha I, resolute divers frequently visited the Spouting Cave, and on one occasion fire, enclosed in a small calabash, was taken down through the whirlpool, with the view of making a light and exploring its mysterious chambers; but the fire was scattered and extinguished by an unseen hand, and those who brought it hastily retreated to escape a shower of rocks sent down upon them from the roof of the cavern. The existence of the cave is still known, and the whirlpool and spouting column marking the entrance to it are pointed out; but longer and longer have grown the intervals between the visits of divers to its sunless depths, until the present generation can point to not more than one, perhaps, who has ventured to enter them.

Tradition has brought down the outlines of a number of supernatural and romantic stories connected with the Spouting Cave, but the nearest complete and most recent of these mookaaos is the legend of Kaala, the flower of Lanai, which is here given at considerably less length than native narration accords it.

It was during an interval of comparative quiet, if not of peace, in the stormy career of Kamehameha I, near the close of the last century, and after the battle of Maunalei, that he went with his court to the island of Lanai for a brief season of recreation. The visit was not made for the purpose of worshipping at the great heiau of Kaunola, which was then half in ruins, or at any of the lesser temples scattered here and there over the little island, and dedicated, in most instances, to fish-gods. He went to Kealia simply to enjoy a few days of rest away from the scenes of his many conflicts, and feast for a time upon the affluent fishing grounds of that locality.

He made the journey with six double canoes, all striped with yellow, and his own bearing the royal ensign. He took with him his war-god, Kaili, and a small army of attendants, consisting of priests, kahunas, kahili and spittoon-bearers, stewards, cooks, and other household servants, as well as a retinue of distinguished chiefs with their personal retainers in their own canoes, and a hundred warriors in the capacity of a royal guard.

Landing, the victorious chief was received with enthusiasm by the five or six thousand people then inhabiting the island. He took up his residence in the largest of the several cottages provided for him and his personal attendants.

Provisions were brought in abundance, and flowers and sweet-scented herbs and vines were contributed without stint. The chief and his titled attendants were garlanded with them. They were strewn in his path, cast at his door, and thrown upon his dwelling, until their fragrance seemed to fill all the air.

Among the many who brought offerings of flowers was the beautiful Kaala, "the sweet-scented flower of Lanai," as she was called. She was a girl of fifteen, and in grace and beauty had no peer on the island. She was the daughter of Oponui, a chief of one of the lower grades, and her admirers were counted by the hundreds. Of the many who sought her as a wife was Mailou, "the bone-breaker." He was a huge, muscular savage, capable of crushing almost any ordinary man in an angry embrace; and while Kaala hated, feared, and took every occasion to avoid him, her father favored his suit, doubtless pleased at the thought of securing in a son-in-law a friend and champion so distinguished for his strength and ferocity.

As Kaala scattered flowers before the chief her graceful movements and modesty were noted by Kaaialii, and when he saw her face he was enraptured with its beauty. Although young in years, he was one of Kamehameha's most valued lieutenants, and had distinguished himself in many battles. He was of chiefly blood and bearing, with sinewy limbs and a handsome face, and when he stopped to look into the eyes of Kaala and tell her that she was beautiful, she thought the words, although they had been frequently spoken to her by others, had never sounded so sweetly to her before. He asked her for a simple flower, and she twined a lei for his neck. He asked her for a smile, and she looked up into his face and gave him her heart.

They saw each other the next day, and the next, and then Kaaialii went to his chief and said: "I love the beautiful Kaala, daughter of Oponui. Your will is law. Give her to me for a wife."

For a moment Kamehameha smiled without speaking, and then replied: "The girl is not mine to give. We must be just. I will send for her father. Come to-morrow."

Kaaialii had hoped for a different answer; but neither protest nor further explanation was admissible, and all he could do was to thank the king and retire.

A messenger brought Oponui to the presence of Kamehameha. He was received kindly and told that Kaaialii loved Kaala and desired to make her his wife. The information kindled the wrath of Oponui. He hated Kaaialii but did not dare to exhibit his animosity before the king. He was in the battle of Maunalei, where he narrowly escaped death at the hands of Kaaialii, after his spear had found the heart of one of his dearest friends, and he felt that he would rather give his daughter to the sharks than to one who had sought his life and slain his friend. But he pretended to regard the proposal with favor, and, in answer to the king, expressed regret that he had promised his daughter to Mailou, the bone-breaker. "However," he continued, "in respect to the interest which it has pleased you, great chief, to take in the matter, I am content that the girl shall fall to the victor in a contest with bare hands between Mailou and Kaaialii."

The proposal seemed to be fair, and, not doubting that Kaaialii would promptly accept it, the king gave it his approval, and the contest was fixed for the day following. Oponui received the announcement with satisfaction, not doubting that Mailou would crush Kaaialii in his rugged embrace as easily as he had broken the bones of many an adversary.

News of the coming contest spread rapidly, and the next day thousands of persons assembled at Kealia to witness it. Kaala was in an agony of fear. The thought of becoming the wife of the bone-breaker almost distracted her, for it was said that he had had many wives, all of whom had disappeared one after another as he tired of them, and the whisper was that he had crushed and thrown them into the sea. And, besides, she loved Kaaialii, and deemed it scarcely possible that he should be able to meet and successfully combat the prodigious strength and ferocity of one who had never been subdued.

As Kaaialii was approaching the spot where the contest was to take place, in the presence of Kamehameha and his court and a large concourse of less distinguished spectators, Kaala sprang from the side of her father, and, seizing the young chief by the hand, exclaimed: "You have indeed slain my people in war, but rescue me from the horrible embrace of the bone-breaker, and I will catch the squid and beat the kapa for you all my days!"

With a dark frown upon his face, Oponui tore the girl from her lover before he could reply. Kaaialii followed her with his eyes until she disappeared among the spectators, and then pressed forward through the crowd and stepped within the circle reserved for the combatants. Mailou was already there. He was indeed a muscular brute, with long arms, broad shoulders, and mighty limbs tattooed with figures of sharks and birds of prey. He was naked to the loins, and, as Kaaialii approached, his fingers opened and closed, as if impatient to clutch and tear his adversary in pieces.

Although less bulky than the bone-breaker, Kaaialii was large and perfectly proportioned, with well-knit muscles and loins and shoulders suggestive of unusual strength. Nude, with the exception of a maro, he was a splendid specimen of vigorous manhood; but, in comparison with those of the bone-breaker, his limbs appeared to be frail and feminine, and a general expression of sympathy for the young chief was observed in the faces of the large assemblage as they turned from him to the sturdy giant he was about to encounter.

The contest was to be one of strength, courage, agility, and skill combined. Blows with the clenched fist, grappling, strangling, tearing, breaking, and every other injury which it was possible to inflict were permitted. In hakoko[1] and moko[2] contests certain rules were usually observed, in order that fatal injuries might be avoided; but in the combat between Kaaialii and Mailou no rule or custom was to govern. It was to be a savage struggle to the death.

Taunt and boasting are the usual prelude to personal conflicts among the uncivilized; nor was it deemed unworthy the Saxon knight to meet his adversary with insult and bravado. The object was not more to unnerve his opponent than to steel his own courage. With the bone-breaker, however, there was little fear or doubt concerning the result. He knew the measure of his own

---

1. Wrestling.
2. Boxing.

prodigious strength, and, with a malignant smile that laid bare his shark-like teeth, he glared with satisfaction upon his rival.

"Ha! ha!" laughed the bone-breaker, taking a stride toward Kaaialii; "so *you* are the insane youth who has dared to meet Mailou in combat! Do you know who I am? I am the bone-breaker! In my hands the limbs of men are like tender cane. Come, and with one hand let me strangle you!"

"You will need both!" replied Kaaialii. "I know you. You are a breaker of the bones of women, not of men! You speak brave words, but have the heart of a coward. Let the word be given, and if you do not run from me to save your life, as I half-suspect you will, I will put my foot upon your broken neck before you find time to cry for mercy!"

Before Mailou could retort the word was given, and with an exclamation of rage he sprang at the throat of Kaaialii. Feigning as if to meet the shock, the latter waited until the hands of Mailou were almost at his throat, when with a quick movement he struck them up, swayed his body to the left, and with his right foot adroitly tripped his over-confident assailant. The momentum of Mailou was so great that he fell headlong to the earth. Springing upon him before he could rise, Kaaialii seized his right arm, and with a vigorous blow of the foot broke the bone below the elbow. Rising and finding his right arm useless, Mailou attempted to grapple his adversary with the left, but a well-delivered blow felled him again to the earth, and Kaaialii broke his left arm as he had broken the right. Regaining his feet, and unable to use either hand, with a wild howl of despair the bone-breaker rushed upon Kaaialii, with the view of dealing him a blow with his bent head; but the young chief again tripped him as he passed, and, seizing him by the hair as he fell, placed his knees against the back of his prostrate foe and broke his spine.

This, of course, ended the struggle, and Kaaialii was declared the victor, amidst the plaudits of the spectators and the congratulations of Kamehameha and the court. Breaking from her father, who was grievously disappointed at the unlooked-for result, and who sought to detain her, Kaala sprang through the crowd and threw herself into the arms of Kaaialii. Oponui would have protested, and asked that his daughter might be permitted to visit her mother before becoming the wife of Kaaialii; but the king put an end to his hopes by placing the hand of Kaala in that of the victorious chief, and saying to him: "You have won her nobly. She is now your wife. Take her with you."

Although silenced by the voice of the king, and compelled to submit to the conditions of a contest which he had himself proposed, Oponui's hatred of Kaaialii knew no abatement, and all that day and the night following he sat alone by the sea-shore, devising a means by which Kaala and her husband might be separated. He finally settled upon a plan.

The morning after her marriage Oponui visited Kaala, as if he had just returned from Mahana, where her mother was supposed to be then living. He greeted her with apparent affection, and was profuse in his expressions of friendship for Kaaialii. He embraced them both, and said: "I now see that you love each other; my prayer is that you may live long and happily together." He then told Kaala that Kalani, her mother, was lying dangerously ill at Mahana, and, believing that she would not recover, desired to see and bless her daughter before she died. Kaala believed the story, for her father wept when he told it, and moaned as if for the dead, and beat his breast; and, with many protestations of love, Kaaialii allowed her to depart with Oponui, with the promise from both of them that she would speedily return to the arms of her husband.

With some misgivings, Kaaialii watched her from the top of the hill above Kealia until she descended into the valley of Palawai. There leaving the path that led to Mahana, they journeyed toward the bay of Kaumalapau. Satisfied that her father was for some purpose deceiving her, Kaala protested and was about to return, when he acknowledged that her mother was not ill at Mahana, as he had represented to Kaaialii in order to secure his consent to her departure, but at the sea-shore, where she had gathered crabs, shrimps, limpets, and other delicacies, and prepared a feast in celebration of her marriage.

Reassured by the plausible story, and half-disposed to pardon the deception admitted by her father, Kaala proceeded with him to the sea-shore. She saw that her mother was not there, and heard no sound but the beating of the waves against the rocks. She looked up into the face of her father for an explanation; but his eyes were cold, and a cruel smile upon his lips told her better than words that she had been betrayed.

"Where is my mother?" she inquired; and then bitterly added: "I do not see her fire by the shore. Must we search for her among the sharks?"

Oponui no longer sought to disguise his real purpose. "Hear the truth!" he said, with a wild glare in his eyes that whitened the lips of Kaala. "The shark shall be your mate, but he will not harm you. You shall go to his home, but he will not devour you. Down among the gods of the sea I will leave you until Kaaialii, hated by me above all things that breathe, shall have left Lanai, and then I will bring you back to earth!"

Terrified at these words, Kaala screamed and sought to fly; but her heartless father seized her by the hand and dragged her along the shore until they reached a bench of the rocky bluff overlooking the opening to the Spouting Cave. Oponui was among the few who had entered the cavern through its gate of circling waters, and he did not for a moment doubt that within its gloomy walls, where he was about to place her, Kaala would remain securely hidden until such time as he might choose to restore her to the light.

Standing upon the narrow ledge above the entrance to the cave, marked by alternate whirlpool and receding column, Kaala divined the barbarous purpose of her father, and implored him to give her body to the sharks at once rather than leave her living in the damp and darkness of the Spouting Cave, to be tortured by the slimy and venomous creatures of the sea.

Deaf to her entreaties, Oponui watched until the settling column went down into the throat of the whirlpool, when he gathered the frantic and struggling girl in his arms and sprang into the circling abyss. Sinking a fathom or more below the surface, and impelled by a strong current setting toward the mouth of the cave, he soon found and was swept through the entrance, and in a few moments stood upon a rocky beach in the dim twilight of the cavern, with the half-unconscious Kaala clinging to his neck.

The only light penetrating the cave was the little refracted through the waters, and every object that was not too dark to be seen looked greenish and ghostly. Crabs, eels, sting-rays, and other noisome creatures of the deep were crawling stealthily among the rocks, and the dull thunder of the battling waves was the only sound that could be distinguished.

Disengaging her arms, he placed her upon the beach above the reach of the waters, and then sat down beside her to recover his breath and wait for a retreating current to bear him to the surface. Reviving, Kaala looked around her with horror, and piteously implored her father not to leave her in that dreadful place beneath the waters.

For some time he made no reply, and then it was to tell her harshly that she might return with him if she would promise to accept the love of the chief of Olowalu, in the valley of Palawai, and allow Kaaialii to see her in the embrace of another. This she refused to do, declaring that she would perish in the cave, or the attempt to leave it, rather than be liberated on such monstrous conditions.

"Then here you will remain," said Oponui, savagely, "until I return, or the chief of Olowalu comes to bear you off to his home in Maui!" Then, rising to his feet, he continued hastily, as he noted a turn in the current at the opening: "You cannot escape without assistance. If you attempt it you will be dashed against the rocks and become the food of sharks."

With this warning Oponui turned and plunged into the water. Diving and passing with the current through the entrance, he was borne swiftly to the surface and to his full length up into the spouting column; but he coolly precipitated himself into the surrounding waters, and with a few strokes of the arms reached the shore.

PART II

Kaaialii watched the departure of Kaala and her father until they disappeared in the valley of Palawai, and then gloomily returned to his hut. His fears troubled him. He thought of his beautiful Kaala, and his heart ached for her warm embrace. Then he thought of the looks and words of Oponui, and recalled in both a suggestion of deceit. Thus harassed with his thoughts, he spent the day in roaming alone among the hills, and the following night in restless slumber, with dreams of death and torture. The portentous cry of an alae roused him from his kapamoe before daylight, and until the sun rose he sat watching the stars. Then he climbed the hill overlooking the valley of Palawai to watch for the return of Kaala, and wonder what could have detained her so long. He watched until the sun was well up in the heavens, feeling neither thirst nor hunger, and at length saw a pau fluttering in the wind far down the valley.

A woman was rapidly approaching, and his heart beat with joy, for he thought she was Kaala. Nearer and nearer she came, and Kaaialii, still hopeful, ran down to the path to meet her. Her step was light and her air graceful, and it was not until he had opened his arms to receive her that he saw that the girl was not Kaala. She was Ua, the friend of Kaala, and almost her equal in beauty. They had been reared together, and in their love for each other were like sisters. They loved the same flowers, the same wild songs of the birds, the same paths among the hills, and, now that Kaala loved Kaaialii, Ua loved him also.

Recognizing Kaaialii as she approached, Ua stopped before him, and bent her eyes to the ground without speaking.

"Where is Kaala?" inquired Kaaialii, raising the face of Ua and staring eagerly into it. "Have you seen her? Has any ill come to her? Speak!"

"I have not seen her, and know of no ill that has befallen her," replied the girl; "but I have come to tell you that Kaala has not yet reached the hut of Kalani, her mother; and as Oponui, with a dark look in his face, was seen to lead her through the forest of Kumoku, it is feared that she has been betrayed and will not be allowed to return to Kealia."

"And that, too, has been my fear since the moment I lost sight of her in the valley of Palawai," said Kaaialii. "I should not have trusted her father, for I knew him to be treacherous and unforgiving. May the wrath of the gods follow him if harm has come to her through his cruelty! But I will find her if she is on the island! The gods have given her to me, and in life or death she shall be mine!"

Terrified at the wild looks and words of Kaaialii, Ua clasped her hands in silence.

"Hark!" he continued, bending his ear toward the valley. "It seems that I hear her calling for me now!" And with an exclamation of rage and despair Kaaialii started at a swift pace down the path taken by Kaala the day before. As he hurried onward, he saw, at intervals, the footprints of Kaala in the dust, and every imprint seemed to increase his speed.

Reaching the point where the Mahana path diverged from the somewhat broader ala of the valley, he followed it for some distance hoping that Ua had been misinformed, and that Kaala had really visited her mother and might be found with her; but when he looked for and failed to find the marks of her feet where in reason they should have been seen had she gone to Mahana with her father, he returned and continued his course down the valley.

Suddenly he stopped. The footprints for which he was watching had now disappeared from the Palawai path, and for a moment he stood looking irres-olutely around, as if in doubt concerning the direction next to be pursued. In his uncertainty several plans of action presented themselves. One was to see what information could be gathered from Kaala's mother at Mahana, another to follow the Palawai valley to the sea, and a third to return to Kealia and consult a kaula. While these various suggestions were being rapidly canvassed, and before any conclusion could be reached, the figure of a man was seen approaching from the valley below.

Kaaialii secreted himself behind a rock, where he could watch the path without being seen. The man drew nearer and nearer, until at last Kaaialii was enabled to distinguish the features of Oponui, of all men the one whom he most desired to meet. His muscles grew rigid with wrath, and his hot breath burned the rock behind which he was crouching. He buried his fingers in the earth to teach them patience, and clenched his teeth to keep down a struggling exclamation of vengeance. And so he waited until Oponui reached a curve in the path which brought him, in passing, within a few paces of the eyes that were savagely glaring upon him, and the next moment the two men stood facing each other.

Startled at the unexpected appearance of Kaaialii, Oponui betrayed his guilt at once by attempting to fly; but, with the cry of "Give me Kaala!" Kaaialii sprang forward and endeavored to seize him by the throat.

A momentary struggle followed; but Oponui was scarcely less powerful than his adversary, and, his shoulders being bare, he succeeded in breaking from the grasp of Kaaialii and seeking safety in flight toward Kealia.

With a cry of disappointment, Kaaialii started in pursuit. Both were swift of foot, and the race was like that of a hungry shark following his prey. One was inspired by fear and the other with rage, and every muscle of the runners was strained. Leaving the valley path, Oponui struck for Kealia by a shorter course across the hills. He hoped the roughness of the route and his better knowledge of it would give him an advantage; but Kaaialii kept closely at his heels. On they sped, up and down hills, across ravines and along rocky ridges, until they reached Kealia, when Oponui suddenly turned to the left and made a dash for the temple and puhonua not far distant. Kaaialii divined his purpose, and with a last supreme effort sought to thwart it. Gaining ground with every step, he made a desperate grasp at the shoulder of Oponui just as the latter sprang through the entrance and dropped to the earth, exhausted within the protecting walls of the puhonua. Kaaialii attempted to follow, but two priests promptly stepped into the portal and refused to allow him to pass.

"Stand out of the way, or I will strangle you both!" exclaimed Kaaialii, fiercely, as he threw himself against the guards.

"Are you insane?" said another long-haired priest, stepping forward with a tabu staff in his hand. "Do you not know that this is a puhonua, sacred to all who seek its protection? Would you bring down upon yourself the wrath of the gods by shedding blood within its walls?"

"If I may not enter, then drive him forth!" replied Kaaialii, pointing toward Oponui, who was lying upon the ground a few paces within, intently regarding the proceedings at the gate.

"That cannot be," returned the priest. "Should he will to leave, the way will not be closed to him; otherwise he may remain in safety."

"Coward!" cried Kaaialii, addressing Oponui in a taunting tone. "Is it thus that you seek protection from the anger of an unarmed man? A pau would better become you than a maro. You should twine leis and beat kapa with women, and think no more of the business of men. Come without the walls, if your trembling limbs will bear you, and I will serve you as I did your friend, the breaker of women's bones. Come, and I will tear from your throat the tongue that lied to Kaala, and feed it to the dogs!"

A malignant smile wrinkled the face of Oponui, as he thought of Kaala in her hiding-place under the sea, but he made no reply.

"Do you fear me?" continued Kaaialii. "Then arm yourself with spear and battle-axe, and with bare hands I will meet and strangle you!"

Oponui remained silent, and in a paroxysm of rage and disappointment Kaaialii threw himself upon the ground and cursed the tabu that barred him from his enemy.

His friends found and bore him to his hut, and Ua, with gentle arts and loving hands, sought to soothe and comfort him. But he would not be consoled. He talked and thought alone of Kaala, and, hastily partaking of food that he might retain his strength, started again in search of her. Pitying his distress, Ua followed him—not closely, but so that she might not lose sight of him altogether.

He travelled in every direction, stopping neither for food nor rest. Of every one he met he inquired for Kaala, and called her name in the deep valleys and on the hill-tops. Wandering near the sacred spring at the head of the waters of Kealia, he met a white-haired priest bearing from the fountain a calabash of water for ceremonial use in one of the temples. The priest knew and feared him, for his looks were wild, and humbly offered him water.

"I ask not for food or water, old man," said Kaaialii. "You are a priest—perhaps a kaula. Tell me where I can find Kaala, the daughter of Oponui, and I will pile your altars with sacrifices!"

"Son of the long spear," replied the priest, "I know you seek the sweet-smelling flower of Palawai. Her father alone knows of her hiding-place. But it is not here in the hills, nor is it in the valleys. Oponui loves and frequents the sea. He hunts for the squid in dark places, and dives for the great fish in deep waters. He knows of cliffs that are hollow, and of caves with entrances below the waves. He goes alone to the rocky shore, and sleeps with the fish-gods, who are his friends. He—"

"No more of him!" interrupted the chief, impatiently. "Tell me what has become of Kaala!"

"Be patient, and you shall hear," resumed the priest. "In one of the caverns of the sea, known to Oponui and others, has Kaala been hidden. So I see her now. The place is dark and her heart is full of terror. Hasten to her. Be vigilant, and you will find her; but sleep not, or she will be the food of the creatures of the sea."

Thanking the priest, Kaaialii started toward the bay of Kaumalapau, followed by the faithful Ua, and did not rest until he stood upon the bluff of Palikaholo, overlooking the sea. Wildly the waves beat against the rocks. Looking around, he could discern no hiding-place along the shore, and the thunder of the breakers and the screams of the sea-gulls were the only sounds to be heard. In despair he raised his voice and wildly exclaimed: "Kaala! O Kaala! where are you? Do you sleep with the fish-gods, and must I seek you in their homes among the sunken shores?"

The bluff where he was standing overlooked and was immediately above the Spouting Cave, from the submerged entrance to which a column of water was rising above the surface and breaking into spray. In the mist of the upheaval he thought he saw the shadowy face and form of Kaala, and in the tumult of the rushing waters fancied that he heard her voice calling him to come to her.

"Kaala, I come!" he exclaimed, and with a wild leap sprang from the cliff to clasp the misty form of his bride.

He sank below the surface, and, as the column disappeared with him and he returned no more, Ua wailed upon the winds a requiem of love and grief in words like these:

"Oh! dead is Kaaialii, the young chief of Hawai'i,
The chief of few years and many battles!
His limbs were strong and his heart was gentle;
His face was like the sun, and he was without fear.
Dead is the slayer of the bone-breaker;
Dead is the chief who crushed the bones of Mailou;
Dead is the lover of Kaala and the loved of Ua.
For his love he plunged into the deep waters;
For his love he gave his life. Who is like Kaaialii?
Kaala is hidden away, and I am lonely;
Kaaialii is dead, and the black kapa is over my heart:
Now let the gods take the life of Ua!"

With a last look at the spot where Kaaialii had disappeared, Ua hastened to Kealia, and at the feet of Kamehameha told of the rash act of the despairing husband of Kaala. The king was greatly grieved at the story of Ua, for he loved the young chief almost as if he had been his son. "It is useless to search for the body of Kaaialii," he said, "for the sharks have eaten it." Then, turning to one of his chiefs, he continued: "No pile can be raised over his bones. Send for Ualua, the poet, that a chant may be made in praise of Kaaialii."

Approaching nearer, Papakua, a priest, requested permission to speak. It was granted, and he said: "Let me hope that my words may be of comfort. I have heard the story of Ua, and cannot believe that the young chief is dead. The spouting waters into which Kaaialii leaped mark the entrance to the cave of Palikaholo. Following downward the current, has he not been drawn into the cavern, where he has found Kaala, and may still be living? Such, at least, is my thought, great chief."

"A wild thought, indeed!" replied the king; "yet there is some comfort in it, and we will see how much of truth it may reveal."

Preparations were hastily made, and with four of his sturdiest oarsmen Kamehameha started around the shore for the Spouting Cave under the bluff of Palikaholo, preceded by Ua in a canoe with Keawe, her brother.

PART III

When Kaaialii plunged into the sea he had little thought of anything but death. Grasping at the spouting column as he descended, it seemed to sink with him to the surface, and even below it, and in a moment he felt himself being propelled downward and toward the cliff by a strong current. Recklessly yielding to the action of the waters, he soon discerned an opening in the submerged base of the bluff, and without an effort was drawn swiftly into it. The force of the current subsided, and to his surprise his head rose above the surface and he was able to breathe. His feet touched a rocky bottom, and he rose and looked around with a feeling of bewilderment. His first thought was that he was dead and had reached the dark shores of Po, where Milu, prince of death, sits enthroned in a grove of kou trees; but he smote his breast, and by the smart knew that he was living, and had been borne by the waters into a cave beneath the cliff from which he had leaped to grasp the misty form of Kaala.

Emerging from the water, Kaaialii found himself standing on the shore of a dimly-lighted cavern. The air was chilly, and slimy objects touched his feet, and others fell splashing into the water from the rocks. He wondered whether it would be possible for him to escape from the gloomy place, and began to watch the movements of the waters near the opening, when a low moan reached his ear.

It was the voice of Kaala. She was lying near him in the darkness on the slimy shore. Her limbs were bruised and lacerated with her fruitless attempts to leave the cave, and she no longer possessed the strength to repel the crabs and other loathsome creatures that were drinking her blood and feeding upon her quivering flesh.

"It is the wailing of the wind, or perhaps of some demon of the sea who makes this horrible place his home," thought Kaaialii.

He feared neither death nor its ministers; yet something like a shudder possessed him as he held his breath and listened, but he heard nothing but the thunder of the breakers against the cavern walls.

"Who speaks?" he exclaimed, advancing a pace or two back into the darkness.

A feeble moan, almost at his feet, was the response.

Stooping and peering intently before him, he distinguished what seemed to be the outlines of a human form. Approaching and bending over it, he caught the murmur of his own name.

"It is Kaala! Kaaialii is here!" he cried, as he tenderly folded her in his arms and bore her toward the opening. Seating himself in the dim light, he pushed back the hair from her cold face, and sought to revive her with caresses and words of endearment. She opened her eyes, and, nestling closer to his breast, whispered to the ear that was bent to her lips: I am dying, but I am happy, for you are here."

He sought to encourage her. He told her that he had come to save her; that the gods, who loved her and would not let her die, had told him where to find her; that he would take her to his home in Kohala, and always love her as he loved her then.

She made no response. There was a sad smile upon her cold lips. He placed his hand upon her heart, and found that it had ceased to beat. She was dead, but he still held the precious burden in his arms; and hour after hour he sat there on the gloomy shore of the cavern, seeing only the pallid face of Kaala, and feeling only that he was desolate.

At length he was aroused by the splashing of water within the cave. He looked up, and Ua, the gentle and unselfish friend of Kaala, stood before him, followed a moment after by Kamehameha. The method of entering and leaving the cave was known to Keawe, and he imparted the information to his sister. Ua first leaped into the whirlpool, and the dauntless Kamehameha did not hesitate in following.

As the king approached, Kaaialii rose to his feet and stood sadly before him. He uttered no word, but with bent head pointed to the body of Kaala.

"I see," said the king, softly; "the poor girl is dead. She could have no better burial-place. Come, Kaaialii, let us leave it."

Kaaialii did not move. It was the first time that he had ever hesitated in obeying the orders of his chief.

"What! Would you remain here?" said the king. "Would you throw your life away for a girl? There are others as fair. Here is Ua; she shall be your wife, and I will give you the valley of Palawai. Come, let us leave here at once, lest some angry god close the entrance against us!"

"Great chief," replied Kaaialii, "you have always been kind and generous to me, and never more so than now. But hear me. My life and strength are gone. Kaala was my life, and she is dead. How can I live without her? You are my chief. You have asked me to leave this place and live. It is the first request of yours that I have ever disobeyed. It shall be the last!"

Then seizing a stone, with a swift, strong blow he crushed in brow and brain, and fell dead upon the body of Kaala.

A wail of anguish went up from Ua. Kamehameha spoke not, moved not. Long he gazed upon the bodies before him; and his eye was moist and his strong lip quivered as, turning away at last, he said: "He loved her indeed!"

Wrapped in kapa, the bodies were laid side by side and left in the cavern; and there to-day may be seen the bones of Kaala, the flower of Lanai, and of Kaaialii, her knightly lover, by such as dare to seek the passage to them through the whirlpool of Palikaholo.

Meles of the story of the tragedy were composed and chanted before Kamehameha and his court at Kealia, and since then the cavern has been known as Puhio-kaala, or "Spouting Cave of Kaala."

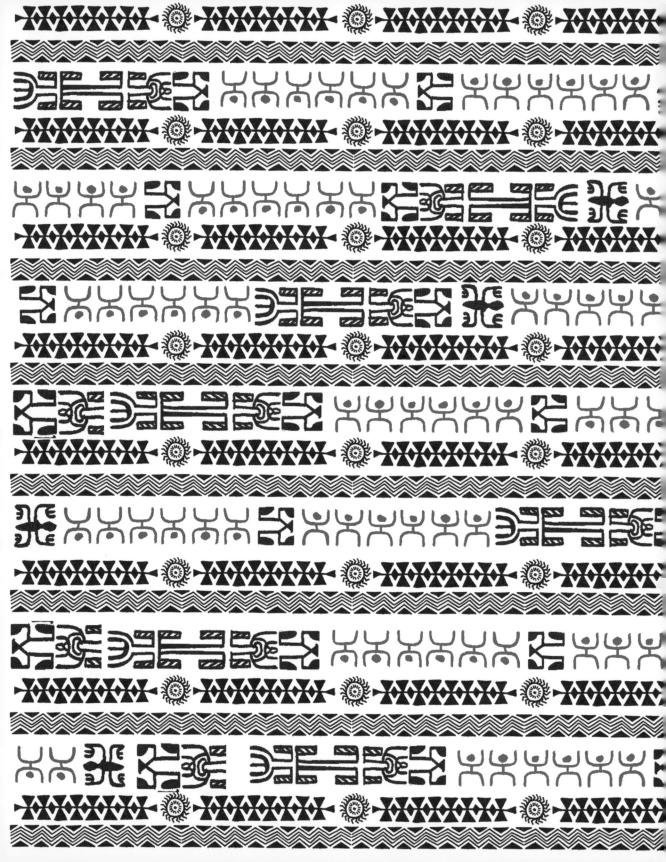

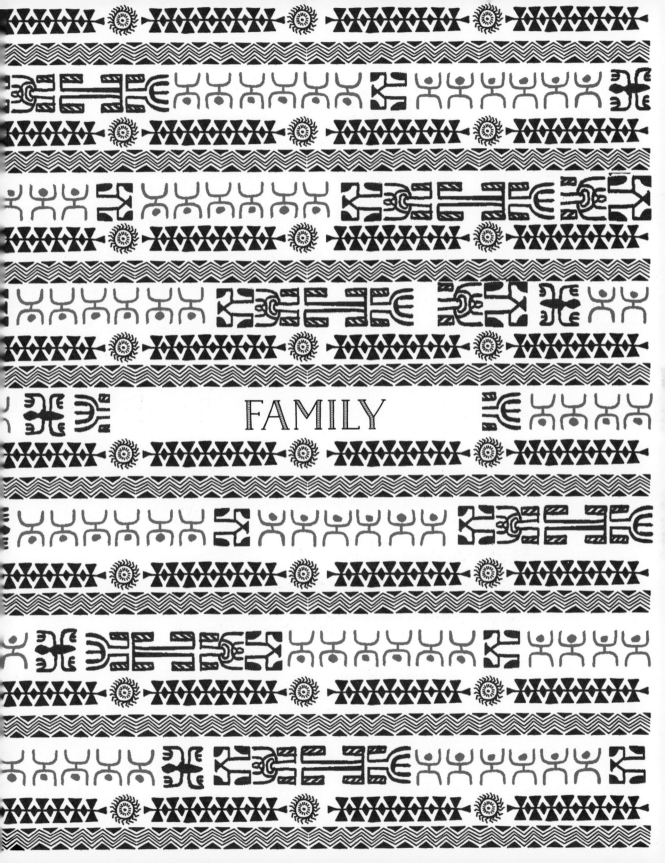

FAMILY

TIGILAU

Samoa

At the time of Tigilau and his Government of Savavau there was a law made by Tigilau that all male children born must be killed but that all female children should live. The reason of this law was that Tigilau was afraid that a boy might be born who was better looking than him. A boy was born to a couple who lived in this district and this boy was killed by Tigilau. This couple then decided that it would be a good idea to go down to the shore and live on a cape running into the sea. They escaped and went to live at this spot and a second son was born to them. They continued to live here until the son had grown to manhood and Tigilau did not know of this boy.

This boy was exceedingly good looking and his name was Seia. The time came when the news of this boy and his beauty was borne on the wind to Tigilau. Tigilau was very angry and he commenced to scheme to bring about the boy's death. A messenger was sent by Tigilau to the place where the boy lived with his parents and the message he carried was that Tigilau desired to see and talk with the boy—when the morning comes, go and call on Tigilau, was the purport of their message. Seia replied that he would do so. The parents of Seia began to cry because they knew that Tigilau would try and kill the boy.

When the day dawned Seia left and, arriving at the malae, he called out, "Tigilau, Tigilau," but Tigilau slept on. He again called out, "Tigilau, what is this business you have with me?"

Everybody then awakened, including the Aualuam.[1] They lifted up the polas or blinds of their houses and saw that Seia was surely a fine looking man. He was dressed in his tapa cloth and necklace and his body was oiled and glistened in the sunlight.

Tigilau said to him, "You were brought here to take away the roots or buttresses of the Toa tree which are obstructing the front of my house."

Seia said, "Very well," and he went to the Toa tree and kicked it on its several sides and the buttresses fell down. Tigilau and his people were surprised at the strength of Seia. Seia then said to Tigilau, "Hold the meeting of Savavau, I will return to the seashore because it is very hot."

This caused Tigilau to be increasingly desirous of bringing about Seia's death. After two days he again sent his messenger to Seia with a request that he for the second time go to Tigilau on important business. For the second time Seia departed at daylight and arrived and stood on the malae and called to Tigilau, who did not awaken. Seia then called out asking what business Tigilau had with him and Tigilau heard him.

Tigilau told Seia that he had been brought for the second time in order to pick breadfruit for the fono of Savavau. This particular breadfruit was a cannibal spirit and if the breadfruit was picked up quickly by the cannibal spirit after it had been knocked down the spirit would then eat the person who went up the tree to get the breadfruit. Seia climbed up the tree and stood in the forked trunk. He reached out with his hand and shook the small branches. All the breadfruit fell down and the cannibal spirit slowly picked them up. No breadfruit remained on the tree; Seia then descended from the tree and called out to Tigilau, "There are the breadfruit for the fono of Savavau—I will return to the shore, as it is hot."

Tigilau was very angry to know that Seia had not been killed and he continued to think up schemes by which to encompass the death of Seia. On the third day he again sent his messenger to Seia. The messenger on arrival at Seia's house called out, "Tigilau again wants you to go to him in the morning

---

1. Single ladies.

to transact some business." The messenger was afraid on this occasion to go to Seia.

Seia again went inland and stood on the malae and called out, but Tigilau did not awaken. He then asked what business Tigilau had with him and Tigilau awakened. He told Seia that he had brought him again to catch the Tanifa[2] for the fono of Savavau.

Seia returned to the shore and went into the sea where there was a large stone jutting out of the water. He sat on this stone and the beach was lined with people who came to watch Seia and to see in what manner he was able to catch the Tanifa. As the sun rose it threw a reflection of Seia on the water and Seia then saw the Tanifa. It was a fearsome sight on account of its size. Seia raised his arm and it cast a picture on the water. The Tanifa made a dash for this shadow and then jumped out of the water. Seia jammed his arm down its throat and pulled it on to the rook and dashed it on to the hard stone until it was dead. Seia then jumped into a canoe and towed the Tanifa ashore.

The people marvelled at the strength of Seia, and Tigilau was very annoyed to learn that he had again escaped his trap. After due consideration he again sent his messenger to Seia with instructions to advise Seia that Tigilau wished to see him early in the morning. As soon as day broke Seia departed from his home and on arrival at the malae of Tigilau called out that he was there and asked what he wanted of him. Tigilau said that he had sent for Seia because he wanted some kava from the bush for the fono of Savavau. Tigilau knew that there was no kava in the bush but he knew that a cannibal lived there and he hoped that Seia would be killed and eaten.

Seia departed in quest of the kava and after travelling a long way through the bush he espied a light. As he approached this light he saw a fine house which was the fale of the cannibal and his wife named Sina. At the time Seia reached the fale the cannibal was absent and only Sina was in evidence. She saw Seia coming and jumped up and asked him where he had come from and why he had come. Seia replied that he had come in search of kava for the

---

2. A large species of shark.

fono of Savavau. Sina told him that there was no kava to be found in the bush and that he should return lest her husband find him there. The name of the cannibal was Uluiva. Seia replied that he would wait until Uluiva returned.

Uluiva returned and as he neared his house he noticed the smell of a stranger. He called out to Sina that there was a strange smell in his house and Sina replied that he was mistaken and that there was no one but herself there. Seia then stood at the door of the house and called out to Uluiva, "You cannot see whether there are any visitors in the house or not."

Uluiva replied that he thought there were visitors and he then entered his house. He laughed when he saw Seia and asked who he was. Seia replied that he was a visitor who wished to fight Uluiva. Uluiva said that Seia was the first stranger who had ever come to his house and he would oblige him by fighting. He told Seia to choose a sword from a number in the house and he, Uluiva, would fight with his rusty sword. Seia asked to have a look at the sword that Uluiva intended fighting with and Uluiva handed it to him. Seia then said, "I will fight with this sword and you can please yourself what weapon you use."

The fight commenced and after a time Uluiva found himself weakening and he said to Seia, "I desire to live and will give you the secret of my strength if you will spare me."

Seia said, "What is this secret?" And Uluiva replied, "It is a wheel which enables me to fly from place to place." Seia then killed the cannibal and planted his body as a "faatiapula."[3]

He then said to Sina, "Come, we will go to the shore." Sina was a very beautiful woman; the two of them rode on the wheel of Uluiva to the seashore. The people of the village saw Seia and Sina coming on the magic wheel and called out in wonderment, "Oh Seia, oh Seia!"

Seia answered them, "Yes, I am Seia the beautiful boy, with the tree roots that I pulled up and the breadfruit that I shook down and the tanifa I killed and the cannibal I killed and planted as a taro top together with Uluiva's wife and his magic wheel."

---

3. A tiapula is a taro top used for replanting.

The magic wheel continued on its way and again was seen by the people who called out, "Oh Seia, oh Seia!" Seia called out, "Yes, I am Seia."

He continued on his way until he arrived at the place where the fono of Seia was being held. As soon as the people saw Seia he called out to them to hold the fono of Savavau and he would return to the shore as it was hot.

The hearts of the parents of Seia were very pleased when they saw him, but Tigilau was very sore because his scheme had again failed to work. He decided that there was only one more trick that he could try and if it failed he would lose everything, including his life. He accordingly sent his messenger to Seia bidding him come to the malae at daybreak, and they would go looking for lovers—they would go to the woman who was living in the west and who was talked about at that time. If this woman accepted one of them the other would be burned in an oven.

The messenger went as instructed and delivered the message of Tigilau to Seia. Seia sent a message back that he agreed but that Tigilau should be the first to try his luck and he would go himself later on in a boat. The messenger returned and explained Seia's message to Tigilau. As soon as day broke, Tigilau with ten boats set out.

Seia told his wife that he would have a sleep but as soon as she saw the boats of Tigilau she must awaken him. Whilst Seia slept Sina commenced to plait his girdle and mix his scented oil and make his necklet. The boats of Tigilau came into sight and Sina awakened Seia. Seia took his magic wheel and fastened it to his boat and with Sina departed to find Tigilau. Seia went first with his boat and waited before the village of the lady they were to make love to.

When the boats of Tigilau arrived he said to Seia, "You will go first to the lady when evening falls." But Seia said, "No, you will go first and if the lady accepts you the oven will be made for me." Tigilau departed when night fell and tried to find the lady but her home was in the heavens and her rest house was below the earth. The party of Tigilau wandered into the rest house of the lady but there was nobody there and Tigilau and his party rushed hither and thither looking for the lady and for the place where she slept. He was not aware that she slept in the heavens.

The cocks began to crow as dawn approached and Tigilau returned to the shore without discovering the lady. When he met Seia he told him that he had not been successful and that it was Seia's turn the following night. Seia replied, "Very well, but I wish to say that it is the custom of this village to place a guard round the lady every second night, and last night when you tried to find her there was no guard."

As evening fell the village lighted torches and stood on guard from the mountain ridge to the reef. Seia lifted up his torn tapa cloth and tied it round his waist and tied up his scented hair in a taro leaf, lest the smell of it make his presence known. He placed his fine tapa cloth and girdle and necklet inside his fishing basket and hung the basket round his neck. He then turned somersaults until he stood on the reef when he cast his fishing net.

Those who were standing guard asked who the man was who fished on forbidden ground. Seia replied that he was fishing because the chiefs had a fancy for fish. The questioners were thus satisfied and wished Seia luck because he was trying to catch fish for their chiefs. Seia continued this trick until he reached the shore, when he donned his fine tapa cloth and necklet and girdle. He then continued to somersault until he stood before the house of the lady desired.

The girls guarding the lady slept in two lines leading from the house and on seeing them, Seia hid. He took off one of the seeds of the pandanus from which his necklet was made and threw it in the direction of the place where the lady slept. She awoke with a start and went to the place where Seia was hidden and asked who it was who had thrown the fala. Seia replied that he was Tigilau and he did this because he wished to know if the lady wanted Tigilau. The lady replied, "If you don't speak the truth and tell me who you are I will call out." The lady then caught hold of the hand of Seia and led him away because she wished Seia to be her husband.

Seia then said, "Come with me, we will go to my boat, which is on the shore, but you must first of all untie the taro leaf from my head." She did so and smelt the scent of the oil on his head. The girls who were supposed to guard the lady awakened and sniffed at the scent in the air and the men on guard right down to the reef also noticed it. Seia then said to his lady, "Hold tight to me," and he turned somersaults until he reached his boat where Sina waited.

He then told them that he was tired and would have a sleep but as soon as day dawned they should jump in the sea and have a bath. It was done as ordered and when day broke the people on the boats of Tigilau saw that there were two girls in the boat of Seia. They awakened Tigilau and he saw that Seia had with him the lady desired. Tigilau then jumped into the sea with his spear and killed himself.

Seia awakened and went off in his boat. His parents saw him as he approached and were delighted to learn that their dear son had once again returned in safety and had successfully overcome all the schemes of Tigilau.

THE STORY of the EARTH

᠄᠄᠄᠄᠄

Samoa

There once lived a couple named Lutane and Lufafine[1] and they had two daughters named Aloaloalela and Sautia. They had as their matai or guardian the Sun. They lived for a great many years and their two daughters were very beautiful.

There came a day when the Sun said to Lufafine and Lutane, "Bring your daughter Aloaloalela, I wish to marry her." The couple replied, "Very well, but let the other daughter who is working also come." The old father then said to his daughter Aloaloalela, "The Sun now comes for you, he has told me to tell you to go to live with him." Aloaloalela then began to cry.

Some time later on she went to live with the Sun and the old couple died. The other daughter Sautia then journeyed to the place where her sister lived with the Sun. Some time later on, Aloaloalela became pregnant and when she told her sister it was suggested that they escape from the Sun. They ran away and jumped into the sea and continued swimming for a long time.

Suddenly Sautia cried out, "Alas, my leg has been bitten off by a shark." Aloaloalela encouraged her to swim on and be strong and they would find a place where the water was shallow and rest.

Some little while later Aloaloalela cried out, "Alas, I am about to give birth to a child." Sautia said, "But there is nowhere when such an event can properly

---

1. Lu the man and Lu the woman.

take place." Aloaloalela then gave birth to nothing but clotted blood in the sea and continued to swim on.

Tagaloaalagi from his place in the sky noticed this blood floating on the ocean and he said to Uatea and Uaale, "Go down below and bring me my son who is floating on the sea." Uatea and Uaale did as ordered and brought the boy up to Tagaloaalagi. As soon as they returned Tagaloaalagi grasped hold of the lifeless mass and alternately blew on it and dipped it into the ocean. The boy suddenly came to life and began to cry.

The girls who had escaped continued to swim on and ultimately found a shallow place in the ocean where they stood up and rested. It was a very small place, but it grew slowly until it was sufficient to become an island and it is a Samoan belief that this first piece of land in the world was the island that is now known as Manua and it became the island of the two ladies who first occupied it, Aloaloalela and Sautia.

The boy who had been saved by Tagaloaalagi continued under his care and grew to manhood. Tagaloaalagi said to him one day, "Go below with my water bottles and fill them for me." The boy went as he was bidden and the tagatia party of the sister of Tagaloaalagi[2] called to him to play also. He stopped and they further explained that if he lost in the game they would have the right to beat him with the stick used in the game, and if they lost, he would enjoy the same right.

The children of the sister of Tuatagaloaalagi threw their stick and it sailed for a long distance through the air. He then took his turn and threw the stick further, thereby winning the privilege of hitting the other boys with his stick. He continued to so treat them, and they began to cry so loudly that the sister heard them and came to see what the trouble was. She saw that the boy continued to thrash her children and she jumped forward and asked him what he meant by thrashing them. He explained that he had thrown the stick further than her boys and thereby won the right to hit them with his throwing stick.

---

2. Children of this sister who played the game of Tagatia which consists of throwing a stick along the ground.

The lady then jumped at the boy and began to thrash him, exclaiming that he was not a real son of Tagaloaalagi and that he was very cruel.

He commenced to cry and then went to fill the water bottles of Tagaloaalagi. When he returned Tagaloaalagi saw that he was crying and asked the reason of his tears. The boy explained what had happened and that the lady had told him that he was not a true son of Tagaloaalagi. He asked Tagaloaalagi to tell him who were his true parents. Tagaloaalagi admitted that he was not his real father and asked him to listen whilst he explained.

He described then how the boy's real mother lived with the Sun and became pregnant and then ran away with her sister and jumped into the sea. He further explained that Aloaloalela gave birth to him whilst swimming and he sent his two sons Uatea and Uaale to carry him up from the sea. He told the boy how he had saved his life and cared for him. He then promised to show him his mother and her sister who had run away. He told him to look down and he would see them.

The boy did so and beheld his mother and her sister down below. He said, "Alas, my poor mother and sister, they are being burned by the Sun and drenched by the rain—let me go down below to them." Tagaloaalagi replied, "Very well, get ready." He then called Uatea and Uaale and told them to conduct the boy to his mother. They did so and the women were startled to see him.

The following conversation then ensued—the boy said to his mother, "Where do you two come from?" and the mother replied, "We ran away from the Sun who was our matai." The boy then asked, "Where is your son?" and the mother replied that she had given birth to a son whilst swimming in the sea with her sister. She was further asked where the son was now, and he received a reply that the mother had left it floating on the surface of the sea.

The boy then said, "I am your son—I was found floating on the surface of the sea by Tagaloaalagi and he sent Uatea and Uaale to pick me up and take me to him. I was brought to life by Tagaloaalagi and cared for by him until the present time. Tagaloaalagi one day told me to go below and fill his water bottles. As I was doing this the children of his sister asked me to join in the game of Tagatia and it was decided that whoever won the game would have the privilege of hitting the other party with his throwing stick. I won and I thrashed the other boys as agreed upon. The mother of the boys heard the cry and came to see what the trouble was. When she discovered me thrashing them she told me I was a bad boy and commenced to thrash me and told me that I was not a true son of Tagaloaalagi. When I returned with the water bottles to Tagaloaalagi I asked him to tell me the truth and he told me that my real father was the Sun and that you were my real mother. I then asked him to let me go to you and here I am, I will return to him and ask him to make your island beautiful."

When the boy returned, Tagaloaalagi asked him what he had come for and the boy replied that he had returned to ask Tagaloaalagi to be kind and make the island of his mother and her sister beautiful and provide them with everything they wanted. Tagaloaalagi promised to do so and sent trees of every kind and rain so that the island became very beautiful, and it has remained so down to the present time.

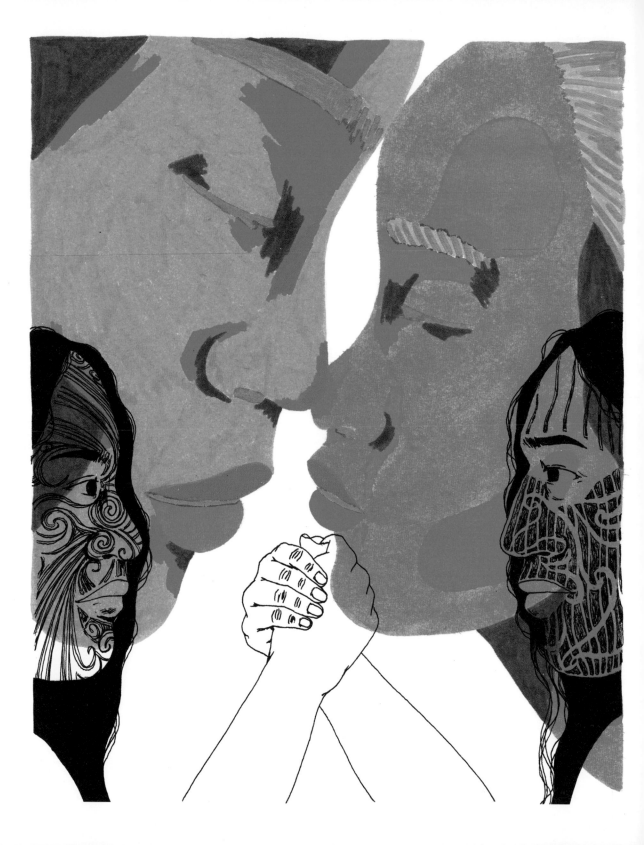

TUNOHOPU'S CAVE:
A TALE of OLD ROTORUA

New Zealand

Green headlands dipping to rocky points, fringed with pohutukawa trees that glow with crimson blossom in midsummer, give topographic charm to the generally low shores of Lake Rotorua. One is romantic Owhata, the ancient home of Hinemoa, she who swam the lake for love of Tutanekai. Another, nearer Rotorua town, is Kawaha Point; eye-resting in its verdure, it is a little over a mile to the westward of the Ohinemutu hotsprings village. The rock-strewn top of the cave is called Te Rangi-Kawhata. On the hilltop are the grassy trenches and ramparts of an ancient fort. At the matarae, the point, with its grey masses of stones, there once was a fishing village. A little way around the point to the north lies a rocky islet covered with shrubs. Near this insulated mass of rhyolite there is a cave with a rock-arched entrance, half-screened by bushes and ferns. It is a story-cave, a refuge place of long ago. The name by which it is known in the hitherto unwritten story of Kawaha is Te Ana-o-Tuno-hopu.[1]

Here, on the lakeshore, two hundred years ago, there lived a chief named Tunohopu, with his wives and children and slaves. The fenced hamlet stood

---

1. Tunohopu's Cave.

133

on the beach, near the point. There were four or five children, one a little boy called Tai-operua.

Just before dawn one morning, the sleeping kainga was aroused by the yells of a band of armed men, a small roving taua of the Ngati-Tuwharetoa tribe from Taupo. The enemy burst into the village and slew most of the people before they had time to seize a weapon or launch a canoe. Most of the Kawaha dwellers happened to have gone across to Mokoia Island, so that Tunohopu had very few of his warriors by his side.

Realising that only instant flight could save him and his children—my Māori narrator did not mention the wives, who were apparently of less account—Tunohopu darted out of his whare, taking his children with him, and made for the water. He snatched up his spear as he jumped from his sleeping mat, and with this he ran one of the enemy through as he left the house. Rushing down to the lake under cover of darkness, he waded out to that rocky islet near the point, carrying two of his children and the others following. Then he and the little ones cautiously waded across to the shore again, and crept into the cave, where they were completely sheltered.

But Tunohopu now discovered that his youngest child, the little boy Tai-operua, was missing. He had been lost in the confusion and was now either dead or a captive. The fugitive family remained in the cave of refuge until their enemies had gone. The Taupo men did not remain long; they set fire to the village and then made off southward. The Mokoia people, on seeing the burning kainga, manned their war-canoes and came dashing across the lake, and the warriors, pursuing the Ngati-Tuwharetoa, came up with the rearguard and killed several men. But most of the raiders got clear away, and they carried with them as a trophy the infant, Tai-operua, slung in a flax basket on a man's back; he was a captive of Tamamutu, the leader of the war party.

Tunohopu sorrowed greatly for his lost child. At last he heard that little Tai-operua was alive and was well treated by Tamamutu at his Taupo home. The father resolved to recover the boy. To have raised a war-party and marched down to the country of Ngati-Tuwharetoa would have pleased him well, but he doubted if that would assist him to regain his child. So, in the year following the raid on Kawaha, Tunohopu set off for Taupo, all alone.

After a journey of more than sixty miles, the father reached the place where Tamamutu's village stood and cautiously reconnoitred it. Outside the fence of the pa, he saw a small boy and asked him, "Where is Tamamutu's house?" The boy directed him to a large carved building in the centre of the village. Tunohopu boldly walked into the village, unnoticed, and, without hesitation, entered the house occupied by the chief. It was walking into the lion's den, for the two tribes were still enemies.

Tamamutu, intensely surprised, and marvelling at his foeman's audacity in venturing alone into the midst of his adversaries, greeted his visitor with the ceremonious politeness of the Māori rangatira. Tunohopu told him why he had journeyed there from Rotorua; he longed for his captive son and had come to recover him or die.

"You shall have your child," said Tamamutu. "But first the tribe must see you and know all about it."

It was near evening, and Tamamutu said he would presently announce Tunohopu's presence to the tribe. "And now," he said, "you must adorn yourself, and attire yourself in fine garments and throw aside those worn pueru which you wore on your long journey from Rotorua, for I wish you to look noble and chieftain-like before your enemies."

So Tunohopu laid aside his tattered flax mats and dressed and oiled his hair and fastened it with a bone heru or comb in the ancient fashion, and in it he placed plumes of the huia bird, the badge of chieftainship, and he girded himself with a finely woven soft flax kilt, and over his shoulders he put a long ornamental bordered black-tasselled cloak of the same material, presented to him by Tamamutu. And then, at his host's request, he stood at the doorway of the house, looking out on the marae, with his taiaha or spear-staff in his hand.

Tamamutu walked out into the marae, the village square, and cried in a loud voice: "He taua e! He taua e!"[2]

---

2. "A war-party! A war-party!"

Instantly the pa was in a commotion. Men seized their spears and clubs and ran to the various kuwaha or gateways of the pa to look for the supposed enemy. No sooner had they had time to gaze around and wonder where the taua was, than Tamamutu, having quickly climbed to the roof of his dwelling, cried: "He taua e! He taua kua uru ki to pa! Tenei e! Tenei kai roto i te whare!"[3]

And when the astonished people rushed up to the chief's house, there they saw their old enemy Tunohopu standing at the doorway, a noble figure in chiefly garb, the emblem of chieftainship adorning his head, and his long, red-plumed taiaha in his hand. Many a warrior would have given battle to the stranger, but he was their chief's guest, and within the shelter of the sacred threshold.

The house was soon crowded with the tribespeople, eager to hear their chief's explanation of Tunohopu's unexpected presence there. Tamamutu addressed them, telling them the reason of the Rotorua warrior's single-handed expedition, and when he had ended, exclamations of admiration and wonder burst from the people.

And then Tamamutu said: "Bring hither Tunohopu's child, that the father may have his son again."

And the little boy was brought in and restored to the father, who wept over his child, and pressed nose to nose in the greeting of the hongi and chanted a song of joy and salutation.

And peace was made between the two tribes. That night Tamamutu and his chief men made orations, in which they declared that there would now be an end of enmity; and Tunohopu said that he was filled with gratitude and love for his late enemies, because of the recovery of his child, who was lost, but now was found.

The visiting chief remained there for many days, an honoured guest of the tribe, and he was mightily feasted and many gifts were given him; and when he left for his home again a retinue of bearers accompanied him to carry loads

---

3. "A war-party! A war-party has entered the village! Here it is, here within the house!"

of preserved birds,[4] the tui, kaka, and pigeon, potted in bark cases hermetically sealed, and other foods of Taupo, as presents for the people of Kawaha.

So happily ended Tunohopu's adventure, and from the brave chief of Kawaha down to his descendant, Taua Tutanekai Haerehuka, who told me this story, there are eight generations of men, and the name of Taua's sub-clan of the Arawa is Ngati-Tunohopu.

4. Manu-huahua.
5. Tunohopu's Cave: A Tale of Old Rotorua

A NOTE ON THE SOURCES

The stories in this book were collected, translated, and published in the late nineteenth and early twentieth centuries. They have been excerpted from the following publications, all of which are in the public domain.

Ahnne, Édouard. *Bulletin de la Société des Études Océaniennes, numéro 46*. Papete Imprimerie du gouvernement, 1933. La bibliothèque scientifique numérique polynésienne. https://anaite.upf.pf/items/show/533#?c=0&m=0&s=0&cv=0

———. *Bulletin de la Société des Études Océaniennes, numéro 68*. Papete Imprimerie du gouvernement, 1940. La bibliothèque scientifique numérique polynésienne. https://anaite.upf.pf/items/show/555#?c=0&m=0&s=0&cv=0

Best, Elsdon. *Maori Religion and Mythology Part 2*. Wellington: Dominion Museum, 1929. New Zealand Electronic Text Collection, P. D. Hasselberg, 1982. https://nzetc.victoria.ac.nz/tm/scholarly/tei-Bes02Reli.html

Cowan, James, and Hon. Sir Maui Pomare, KBE, CMG, MD, MP. *Legends of the Maori*. Wellington: Whitcombe and Tombs/Harry H. Tombs, 1930–34. New Zealand Electronic Text Collection, Southern Reprints, 1987. http://nzetc.victoria.ac.nz/tm/scholarly/tei-Pom01Lege-t1-front-d1-d1.html

Grey, Sir George. *Polynesian Mythology and Ancient Traditional History of the New Zealand Race, as Furnished by Their Priests and Chiefs*. London: John Murray, 1855. Internet Archive, 2017. https://archive.org/details/in.ernet.dli.2015.219427/page/n3/mode/2up

His Hawai'ian Majesty King David Kalakaua. Edited by Hon. R. M. Daggett. *The Legends and Myths of Hawai'i: The Fables and Folk-Lore of a Strange People*. New York: Charles L. Webster, 1888. Internet Archive, 2011. https://archive.org/details/legendsmythsofha00kala/page/n13/mode/2up

Thrum, Thomas G. *Hawaiian Folk Tales: A Collection of Native Legends*. Chicago: A. C. McClurg, 1907. Internet Archive, 2008. https://archive.org/details/Hawai'ianfolktale00thru/page/n14/mode/2up

Tuvale, Te'o. *An Account of Samoan History Up to 1918*. New Zealand Electronic Text Collection, Public Library of New South Wales, 1968. http://nzetc.victoria.ac.nz/tm/scholarly/tei-TuvAcco.html

In most cases, the authors either completed the transcription and translation themselves or worked with unnamed interpreters. The storytellers also generally go unnamed. There are a few exceptions where we have more information, outlined below.

Sir George Grey, according to the *Dictionary of New Zealand Biography*, worked closely with the Ngāti Rangiwewehi leader, scholar, and public servant Te Rangikāheke, but did not credit him in his book.

James Cowan and Hon. Sir Maui Pomare credit "Tunohopu's Cave" to the storyteller Taua Tutanekai Haerehuka.

His Hawai'ian Majesty King David Kalakaua acknowledges the contributions of HRH Liliuokalani; General John Owen Dominis; His Excellency Walter M. Gibson; Professor W. D. Alexander; Mrs. E. Beckley, government librarian; Mr. W. James Smith, secretary of the National Board of Education; and Hon. Abram Fornander to his book.

Thomas G. Thrum credits "Kalelealuaka" to Dr. N. B. Emerson and "Ahuula" and "The Shark-Man, Nanaue" to Mrs. E. M. Nakuina.

Édouard Ahnne traces "The Origin of the Name of Punaauia" back to Peue, a chief of Fautaua, via Teuira Henry and Cecil Lewis. He credits "The Legend of Ruanui" and "The Legend of Paihe Otuu" to Rev. J. M. Orsmond.

Very few adjustments have been made to the original texts for this edition, except for clarity and consistency of punctuation. In one story, "Kalelealuaka," a primary character is referred to throughout as a "cripple." We have eliminated the use of this now-offensive term by referring to the character by his given name (Maliuhaaino) or his occupation (marshal) instead.

The original story "The Legend of Rata" contains a second part about the protagonist's son, which was cut for this edition.

The three Tahitian stories were originally published in French and have been translated for this edition by Mirabelle Korn.

SOURCES

Ahuula: A Legend of Kanikaniaula and the First Feather Cloak
From *Hawaiian Folk Tales: A Collection of Native Legends* by Thomas G. Thrum.

The Art of Netting Learned by Kahukura from the Fairies
From *Polynesian Mythology and Ancient Traditional History of the New Zealand Race, as Furnished by Their Priests and Chiefs* by Sir George Grey.

The Great Battle between the Fish Tribes and Man; How Fish Gained Their Peculiar Forms
From *Maori Religion and Mythology Part 2* by Elsdon Best.

Kaala, the Flower of Lanai: A Story of the Spouting Cave of Palikaholo
From *The Legends and Myths of Hawai'i: The Fables and Folk-Lore of a Strange People* by His Hawai'ian Majesty King David Kalakaua.

Kalelealuaka
From *Hawaiian Folk Tales: A Collection of Native Legends* by Thomas G. Thrum.

The Legend of Paihe Otuu (originally published as La Légende de Paiheotuu)
From *Bulletin de la Société des Études Océaniennes, numéro 46* by Édouard Ahnne.

The Legend of Rata: His Adventures with the Enchanted Tree and Revenge of His Father's Murder
From *Polynesian Mythology and Ancient Traditional History of the New Zealand Race, as Furnished by Their Priests and Chiefs* by Sir George Grey.

The Legend of Ruanui (originally published as La Légende de Ruanui)
From *Bulletin de la Société des Études Océaniennes, numéro 46* by Édouard Ahnne.

The Origin of the Name of Punaauia (originally published as Origine du nom de Punaauia)
From *Bulletin de la Société des Études Océaniennes, numéro 68* by Édouard Ahnne.

The Shark-Man, Nanaue
From *Hawaiian Folk Tales: A Collection of Native Legends* by Thomas G. Thrum.

The Story of Pili and Sina
From *An Account of Samoan History Up to 1918* by Te'o Tuvale.

The Story of the Earth
From *An Account of Samoan History Up to 1918* by Te'o Tuvale.

Tigilau
From *An Account of Samoan History Up to 1918* by Te'o Tuvale.

Tunohopu's Cave: A Tale of Old Rotorua
From *Legends of the Maori*
by James Cowan and Hon. Sir Maui Pomare, KBE, CMG, MD, MP.

The Two Sorcerers
From *Polynesian Mythology and Ancient Traditional History of the New Zealand Race, as Furnished by Their Priests and Chiefs* by Sir George Grey.